Doughnuts, Dreams and Drama Queens

by Leila Rasheed

The
Theatrical
Third Diary
of
Bathsheba
Clarice de Trop

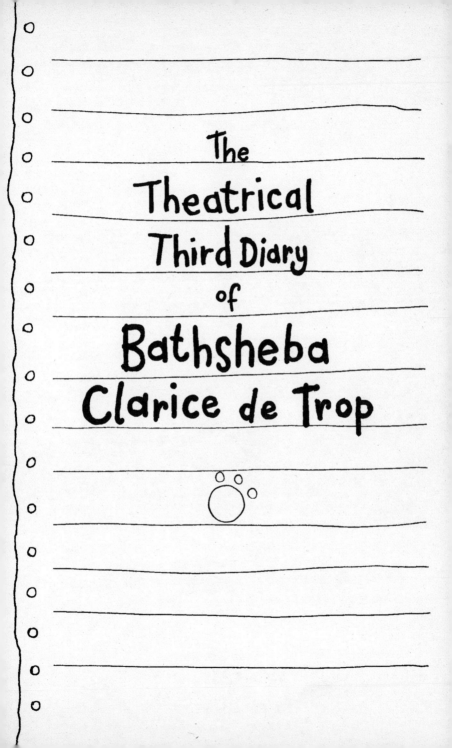

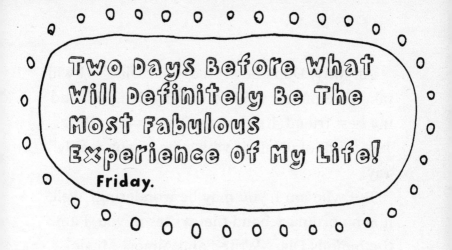

Two Days Before What Will Definitely Be The Most Fabulous Experience Of My Life!

Friday.

Dear new Diary, which Mother sent me all the way from America...

Howdy! Welcome to Clotborough, UK.

You must be so excited to be abroad, dear Diary. And maybe a little scared, too, because of being in a strange country, where tomato is not said "tomato," but "tomato." Oh, that doesn't really work when you write it down. I mean, I say "toe-mah-toe," you say "ta-may-toe." Only you don't, since you are a diary and can't talk.

Anyway! Don't be scared, dear Diary – I will take care of you. And so will my dad, Bill, and my best friend, Keisha, and her mother, Bev. Just think of us all as your new, happy family! Yay!

But who am I, you may be wondering? Well, it is no ordinary hand that writes in you. I am the famous Diary-Writer, and Almost-Movie-Star, Bathsheba Clarice de Trop. Ta-dah!

Actually to be totally completely honest, I am not very famous yet. In fact, I am not famous at all yet. But! That is all going to change, because the day after tomorrow I am going somewhere very special and exciting.

Guess where I'm going! I'll give you a clue – it's a place where dreams are made and stars are born and fame is just a photograph away (tra la!).

No, not Hollywood. Although that's where Mother is right now, and where the movie *Bathsheba Superstar*, which is sort of about me, is being made. Actually it is more about the not-real Bathsheba, who is the magnificent heroine of all the books that Mother writes. What I mean is, although that Bathsheba is named after me, the movie is really entirely about her and actually not about me at all. Sigh.

Maybe I should tell you a little about me, DD (aka Dear Diary), since you're new. Well, I myself am just ordinary. But my mother is a super-successful writer of children's books! Yes, that's right. She writes the BATHSHEBA series. These – as you probably know if you have ever been anywhere near a bookstore – are all about a character, as I said, with the same name as me: Bathsheba Clarice de Trop. But the fictional Bathsheba is not ordinary at all. She is Highly Glam, and head of everything in her super-exclusive school, and she is always having sophisticated sleepovers with her royal best friends, or else saving the world, if it's daytime.

Last year, a Hollywood film company decided to make a movie of Mother's books. It is called BATHSHEBA SUPERSTAR! I did think that they might let me play Bathsheba – since my Destiny is to be a famous Movie Star – but they gave the part to a horrible show-offy actress named Avocado Dieppe instead.

Because of the movie, Mother went to live in Hollywood for a year, to Network. I was going to go with her, but then...well, everything changed. I wrote about it in the first diary I ever had, which I actually called Chips, Beans and Limousines, but basically my Long-Lost Dad turned up, and I ended up going to live with him instead. He was Long-Lost for six years, and I only really got to know him this year, so sometimes I call him Bill, which is his first name, instead of Dad. But I love him the same whatever I call him!

Oh, and Bill and Mother aren't together. Which is a very good thing really since they would be sure to split up instantly if they were together, because they are TOTALLY different people. They are actually so different that I sometimes wonder how they managed to have me in the first place!

Anyway. Where was I?

Oh yes!

THE MOST FABULOUS EXPERIENCE OF MY LIFE!!

SQUEEEEEE!!!!!

So, it's not Hollywood. But it's the next best place to Hollywood.

No, not Bollywood either! Give up guessing? Okay, I'll tell you.

Dear Diary, you and me are on our way to DRAMARAMA CAMP!!!

Dramarama ta-dah tra-la-la camp!!!

Yes yes yes yes yes yes yes!

Oh, hang on, maybe you don't know what that is, because you have only just arrived from Over The Pond (which means the Atlantic Ocean, which is actually a big pond with whales in it). Luckily, I know the brochure by heart, because I've read it so many times. This is what it says:

Dramarama camp is a prestigious (that means "important," dear Diary) vacation camp for aspiring actors and actresses between the ages of 11 and 16. The children taking part in Dramarama camp come from all over the world for two weeks of hard work, fun and new experiences. As a grand finale they stage an evening show, directed by the Dramarama Director.

The camp is split into two phases.

Week One: intensive drama training from Britain's best performers, supported by young and enthusiastic drama students (the Dramarama Assistants). Working on a theme chosen by the Dramarama Director, the students learn new skills and gain confidence as performers.

Week Two: the public gets to see what goes on at Dramarama camp, as TV cameras for the hit reality show, *Dramarama Diaries*, arrive, together with a mystery guest star. (Squeeee!) The mystery guest star is from the world of showbusiness and helps the students prepare for their final show, which will be staged in the camp theater. *Dramarama Diaries* has launched the careers of many young stars of stage and screen. (Eek! That could be me, this year, dear Diary!)

A typical day at Dramarama camp starts with breakfast at 8 a.m., before the children go on to activities from 9 a.m. until 1 p.m., with a mid-morning break and snack. At 1 p.m. there is lunch, followed by activities from 2 p.m. until 5 p.m., again with a mid-afternoon break and snack. The children have a chance to relax for an hour before dinner at 6 p.m. This may be followed by meetings to organize the final performance, or the children may choose to relax, or work on preparing for the final performance. Bedtime – with lights strictly out! – is at 9 p.m. for younger children, 10 p.m. for older ones.

The second week of camp, when the *Dramarama Diaries* cameras and the mystery guest star are present, is usually geared toward rehearsals for the all-important final performance. This traditionally takes place on the last Saturday evening. Parents are very welcome to attend, and may take their children home after the performance or on Sunday as convenient.

On the front of the brochure is a big picture of Thespia Hall, which is the castle where Dramarama camp happens. Well, it's not really a castle – it's a big old house, but made to look like a castle. Right behind it is a new building with curved walls, which is the theater. Ooh, dear Diary, I am so EXCITED I can hardly sit still! I can't believe I'm really going to spend two whole weeks there!

Bill keeps telling me to just relax and enjoy myself, but dear Diary, this is my Big Chance! If I'm good, then *Dramarama Diaries* will show me on television, and I might even get talent-spotted! How can anyone relax when they know their entire future depends on the next two weeks?!

And do you know what the most fabuliciously excellent part of all is? I'm not going by myself! And not even just with you, dear Diary – though of course you are very important too. No, my best friend is coming with me! Keisha!

She's the nicest person in the world, and she is the best best friend in the world. She sticks up for me like a lioness. And, what is *really* good is that she has been to Dramarama camp before! Yes, because she is an Acting Genius (much better than me). So I won't have to worry about being alone and feeling nervous in a strange new place, because Keisha will be right there with me. We have matching suitcases, and matching pink Superstar sunglasses, which are actually shaped like stars, one for each eye. We are going to wear them to make our Grand Entrance, when we are the first, or one of the first to arrive tomorrow. We have been planning and packing for ages. Keisha is here right now, in fact – she is busy trying on my tops to see if any of them go with her new jeans.

We have made a list of things we have TO DO at Dramarama camp. This is how it goes:

☆ Make a swishingly sashaying starry ENTRANCE arm in arm!

☆ Snag beds right next to each other in one of the big DORMS (ooh, I do like that word, it's so much better than "bedroom"!) so we can meet lots of people and make lots of new friends.

☆ Work hard at every single workshop and make the Mystery Guest Star really impressed with our acting talent.

☆ GET NOTICED by the cameras from Dramarama Diaries! (Last year, two children got spotted and now they're acting in the West End!)

Keisha brought me the latest issue of Young Fame! magazine, which is our favorite read ever because of all the in-depth interviews with real Hollywood actors and actresses, which is just what I want to be. Usually we go in together to buy it, and then we take turns reading it, and then we cut out the parts we like and stick them on our walls. This week there was an interview with Connie Clyde, who's one of my favorite actresses. (She has the most amazing red hair!) Keisha was reading it first.

"Ooh, it says here that Connie rocketed to stardom after being spotted acting in a Shakespeare play in her hometown of Boondocks, Mass.," she told me.

"Shakespeare? Yuck!" I made a face. "Do you remember when Miss Kinsey took us to see that Shakespeare play, *Hamlet*? It went on for three hours, nothing happened, then everyone killed each other – WHY???"

"I think *Hamlet* is really good actually," said Keisha, "especially the subtext."

(Keisha does sometimes say things like that, dear Diary. She can't help it. She is just good at everything, including being brainy.)

"Anyway," she went on, "this wasn't *Hamlet*, it was *A Midsummer Night's Dream*, and she was playing Titania, Queen of the Fairies."

I cut out the most interesting part of the interview, dear Diary, so here it is:

Interviewer: So, how lucky were you to be talent-spotted by a leading theatrical agent?!

Connie Clyde: It wasn't luck – it was destiny, and determination.

Interviewer: What do you mean?

Connie Clyde: Well, it's so important to get the perfect part. A role you can really shine in! My agent said that she got a shiver down her spine when she heard me speaking Titania's lines, and that was how she knew I was special.

Interviewer: Wow... You even turned down other offers to focus on that one role, didn't you?

Connie Clyde: That's right. The minute I read Titania's lines, I knew I was BORN to play Shakespeare's Queen of Fairies.

Ooh, that's the doorbell! Back soon, dear Diary! Try not to miss me!

An awful, awful hour later.

Oh, Diary.

The worst thing in the world has happened.

Maybe there are worse things that could happen, but I don't want to think about them.

I feel as if my middle has been taken away. Sort of floaty. Bill says it's shock. He has given me a cup of hot sweet tea and wrapped me up in a blanket with a hot water bottle.

After drinking tea — I feel calmer now. *

I will try and write this very quickly so I don't have to think about it.

It was Bev at the door. She's Keisha's mother. And she had bad, bad, BAD news.

Keisha can't come to Dramarama camp. But that's not even the BAD news. The bad news – which makes not going to Dramarama camp feel like it's not even *important* – is that the reason she can't come is because her granny in France is really sick and is in the hospital.

She might...she might not get well again.

Bev and Keisha have to fly to France first thing tomorrow so they can see her.

Oh, I feel so worried. So upset!

Poor, poor Keisha and poor, poor Bev!

Keisha cried. Bev didn't, but you could see she had, and that's awful because she is usually such a round, smiley person. It's all WRONG for Bev to be upset.

My pink Superstar sunglasses are sitting on the desk, looking lost and lonely. I can't imagine wearing them. I can't even imagine going to Dramarama camp! How can I have fun when my best friend is so worried?

But I have to. And here's why.

When Keisha told me what had happened I didn't know what to say, dear Diary. I just stared at her wildly. And then she started crying, so I hugged her.

"I won't go to Dramarama camp!" I cried. "I'll come with you to France and take care of you!"

Keisha sniffed and dried her tears and said,

"NO, Bath! I want you to go to Dramarama camp!"

"But how can I, without you?" I wailed.

She took me by the shoulders, and gave me a little shake, but in a nice way.

"I want you to go to Dramarama camp, and I want you to be the best there and I want you to make me proud! I want you to write telling me everything that happens, so I have something happy to read. And I want to come back to England to see you on the front page of Young Fame!, as Dramarama's newest star! You can do it, Bath! If I can't go, it's the next best thing for you to go and tell me all about it." And then she started crying again, and said, "Oh, I hope Granny gets well..."

So then of course I gave her another hug, and I sat there hugging her and wishing I could think of something to say that would make it better, but I couldn't, dear Diary, I couldn't think of ANYTHING!

Later. *

Bill says I can help Keisha by showing her I care about her and writing her lots of letters from Dramarama camp. I can't e-mail her, because her granny doesn't have a computer. I could text too, but you can't say much in a text.

But helping is not the same as making it better.

Oh, Diary, I think the worst feeling in the world is when your friend is sad and you can't do anything – anything at all – to make it all right!

The middle of the night — I can't sleep...

Just a few hours ago I felt all calm and happy

and now it feels as if someone has come along and stirred everything inside me up with a horrible spiky stick.

I can't stop thinking about Keisha, and worrying about her granny. And yet – at the same time – there is still a tiny little squeak of excitement inside me because I am going to Dramarama camp the day after tomorrow.

Is that really selfish of me, dear Diary?

I feel as if I shouldn't be excited when Keisha is so unhappy.

And what will it be like, going to Dramarama camp without Keisha?

I am sort of worried that it will be really different going alone than going with my best friend, who has already been there once and knows all about it and has matching sunglasses with me.

What if I don't Sashay into Dramarama camp, but Creep Nervously in instead?

The cameras will never film me if I Creep.

But how can I Sashay without Keisha?

Oh dear, dear Diary.

Well, at least I get to see Keisha one more time before she goes. Me and Bill are giving her and Bev a lift to the airport tomorrow.

o   o   o   o   o   o   o   o   o

One Day Before I Go
To Dramarama Camp.
Alone...
Saturday.

Dear Diary,

I am finishing my packing.

Oh, it feels so different from yesterday. Then, every time I put something exciting into the suitcase (like, not socks, but for example my new sparkly top) I would think, *Ooh! In just two days I will be wearing this at Dramarama camp, with Keisha!*

But now...

I think I have packed a few tears along with everything else.

This morning me and Bill drove Keisha and

Bev to the airport. Bill has bought a new car. Well, it's not new really, it's old. I mean, it is new for us, but it is actually old for itself. I think it's a little like a very old dog that now and then gets tired and wants to sit down. I said so when we were driving, and Bill said it had better not try and sit down when we are on the highway, or he will have something to say to the man at Clotborough Used Cars which is where he bought it. It was a joke, but none of us could manage to laugh.

At the airport it was busy and we had to wait in line with millions of people all rushing around with their luggage and passports and stuff. And it was horrible because all those people were going off in their pink sun hats and yellow flip-flops to have FUN, FUN, FUN and Bev and Keisha weren't.

Me and Keisha sat on the cart. We didn't talk much, but we *thought* a lot. When your best friend is best enough, you can hear them thinking. Not always *what* they're thinking. But you can tell *if* they are thinking, and not just, for example, letting their mind run on about the possibility of ice cream for dessert or whether maybe unicorns really do exist on a distant planet or under the sea.

I said: "I'll write to you lots, Keisha. I'll write every day. I'll start this afternoon."

Keisha gave me a wobbly smile.

"I'll really look forward to your letters! And hey, I bet you have a great time, and you get the best part, and everyone notices you've got Star Quality! They will," she added, "as soon as they see your pink Superstar sunglasses."

And then it was time for them to go and get on the plane. And I cried a little. And then me and Bill went home.

Oh, there goes the phone.

Five minutes later.

It was Rafiq. Again. He's worried about Keisha. Rafiq is Keisha's boyfriend, but his parents don't approve, so he couldn't come and see her off with me. He's okay, but he's not very good at talking about anything except basketball. And Keisha, of course.

It was nice of him to call.

Bill is being super nice. He said that I shouldn't worry too much and he was sure that Keisha's granny would get better. And at the airport he bought me lots and lots of stamps and some cute notepaper so I can write to Keisha as much as I want. And after the airport he drove to the park café and we had chips and beans for lunch, which usually cheers us up. It is hard to be sad with a chip.

Bill said, "Look at us two, comfort eating! Good thing Bev can't see us..." But that just made us both sob a bit, because Bev is always going on about Comfort Eating and how it is a Bad Thing (for her, anyway).

Half an hour later, sitting on my suitcase, hoping it will not burst.

Okay, dear Diary, I have finished my packing for Dramarama camp – sort of. There are still three pairs of shoes and my extra tutu to go in. And a pajama case in the shape of an elephant. And all my clean underwear that I was going to fit in the cracks, but there were no cracks after all.

Anyway, I am tired of packing – it is
like doing a very hard jigsaw puzzle that
keeps popping open and spilling the pieces
everywhere. So I am not doing anymore right
now. I am going to write a letter to Keisha
instead.

My bedroom
Home
England

Dear Keisha!
How are you? Are you drinking lots of
water and doing foot exercises like you
should on planes? I hope you are! I hope
you are not feeling sad, either.
   I am. Feeling sad, I mean. I am missing
you already!
   Promise you won't be angry, but I am
<u>still</u> excited about going to Dramarama
camp. Even without you. I hope that isn't

really selfish of me. I miss you LOTS AND
LOTS. I WISH you were here. I don't feel like
wearing my pink Superstar sunglasses now
you're not here to wear yours too.

By the way, did you take yours with you? I
think they would really cheer up your granny!
I think she would love to see you in them
and maybe she would be so cheered up she'd
get well at once! Please give her a hug from
me – well, if you think it's okay to do that.
I mean, she doesn't know me, so maybe just
give her the hug and then tell her who it's
from later on if it seems like a good idea.

Anyway, dear Keisha, I will stop now
because nothing much has really happened
since I saw you – oh yes, except Rafiq
called and asked if you were all right.
Oh, and we had chips and beans, but it
was no fun without you. And I sort of
finished packing.

Well, that's all, dear Keisha. I will really stop now!

Lots of love from your bestest bestie,

Bathsheba Clarice de Trop

After dinner.

Well, guess what, dear Diary! I am going to go to Dramarama camp INCOGNITO. Which means under a stage name, like a spy.

We were just eating our soup when Bill put down his spoon and said: "What with all this upset, I totally forgot to tell you I've been on the phone with the Dramarama camp Director, Mrs. Howard."

I clinked my spoon nervously. He sounded very serious.

"Basically, she pointed out to me that you have a very well-known name – you know, what with your famous mother naming the heroine of her best-selling books after you. Everyone at Dramarama camp is going to know who you are at once."

"That would be fun!" I said excitedly.

"It might be. But it might be really stressful, too. It hasn't all been smooth sailing at school, has it?"

That's true, dear Diary. Some people have been really horrible to me, just because of Mother. And some people have really sucked up to me, for the same reason, which is even worse. I don't know why some people do one and some do the other. Keisha says it is all up to their individual psycho-lolly-gy.

"Well, Mrs. Howard suggested – and I think she's right – that it might be best if you attended the camp under an alias."

"An alias? You mean like a stage name?"

"Yes, I suppose so."

Me and Keisha make lists of our favorite names. I thought of some of them. Dewdrop is a good name. So is Trelawny. So is Otis.

"I thought –" Bill blushed – "if you wanted to, of course, you could call yourself by my name."

"What, *Bill*?"

"No, my surname! Smithee. You could be Bathsheba Smithee."

"Bathsheba Smithee," I said slowly. It sounded pretty good! So that's what I'm going to be called at Dramarama camp. It will be like being a spy on a secret mission. And I can always say my middle name is Trelawny.

Okay, now I am going to figure out how to get there. I have to make sure everything is planned. I don't want anything to go wrong!

Bedtime.

Huh, Bill is not being very helpful!

I found him clipping his toenails in the bathroom. Bits of toenail were flying off and pinging into the bathtub (yuckketty!).

"Dramarama camp is very far away," I said, waving the *Driver's Atlas* at him, "so we had better start early."

Bill said, "That's right. Have you packed your shoes?" (Clip – *ping*.)

I moved hastily on, because I have not actually gotten them to fit in the suitcase yet. I am hoping that overnight the suitcase will stretch a little or the contents will settle (like cornflakes when you get less in the box than you hoped for) and so there will be more space.

"I have checked the route on the map," I told him, "and I think we should get up at five o'clock to be sure to get there on time."

Bill put down the clippers.

"Good grief, Bath, we're only going to Yorkshire. We won't need twelve hours to get there." He looked at the map. I had very carefully spent lots of time marking all the most direct roads with a highlighter, dear Diary, because I like to Plan Ahead.

"Bath, these are B roads, country lanes some of them. We'll go straight up the highway and turn right at Leeds, straight there."

"But—"

"And I am not getting up at five, it's completely unnecessary. Seven will do fine."

"But I'll be late!!"

"Nonsense," he said, HEARTLESSLY. And went on cutting his toenails: clip, *ping*.

Later. ♡
　　　　＊

I think he is being really horrible!

Can't he see how important it is to be at

Thespia Hall on time?

He is just lazy, not wanting to get up at five. Mother gets up at five all the time to do her Power Yoga. It can't be that hard!

Later still.

Ooh!

I have a stunning plan!

Back in a moment, dear Diary.

Heh, heh, heh.

After sneakily carrying out a stunning plan.

Ha ha! I have secretly changed Bill's alarm clock while he was in the bathroom. I have changed it from seven to five! He will never know. I WILL get to Dramarama camp on time!

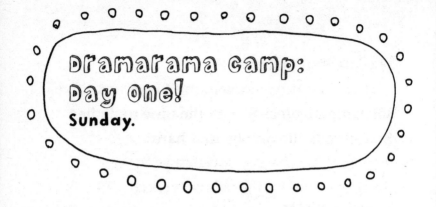

Dramarama Camp: Day One!
Sunday.

5:00 a.m.

Gllurrrrgggghhh...
What day is it?
Is it even a day?

5:02 a.m.

Oooooo!
It is DRAMARAMA CAMP DAY!!!!

5:30 a.m. ♭ *

Bill came staggering out of his bedroom like the Abominable Snowman and fell into the shower. When he got downstairs he kept blinking at the windows and saying, "Why is it still so dark?" and, "Why am I still so tired?"

Oops, dear Diary. I feel a little guilty.

Actually, very guilty.

5:45 a.m. 6 ☆

Bill turned on the radio and discovered that it was not 7:45 a.m. but 5:45 a.m. I am in BIG trouble. And he says it would be even bigger if I wasn't about to go away for a whole two weeks.

Anyway, I am being punished by having to make lots and lots of coffee and keep pouring it into Bill's mug as fast as he drinks it.

He does look as if he has been buried and then dug up again. I told him that, and he said all grown-ups look like that at five in the morning.

I said, "Mother doesn't. Mother always looks perfect."

He muttered something about Mother not being entirely human.

Time for more coffee, I think, dear Diary.

Finally, finally, finally...

I am on my way!!!

I am writing this on the M1, which is the road we are on. We have been driving for about two hours already but most of it was being stuck in traffic. We have actually left London now though!

I am really excited. I keep bouncing up and down in the car and Bill keeps telling me to sit quietly or I'll make myself carsick, but there is NO WAY I could possibly be sick today. I even bought a packet of Gooey Gums at a gas station and I've been eating them and I don't feel sick at all.

Five minutes later.

I have made a big sign that says I AM GOING TO DRAMARAMA CAMP TO BE FAMOUS and put it in the car window.

I wonder where Keisha is now? Will she be at the hospital yet? I hope her granny is getting better!

Ten minutes later.

Oh dear. Bill got really nervous because so many people were honking their horns. He

☆ **41** ☆

thought there was something wrong with
the car.

He was not happy when I told him it was
probably just my sign making people friendly.
He made me take it down. Huh!

He also says will I PLEASE stop shrieking
every time I see a cow, because it is driving
him up the wall.

I said, "Not up the wall, up the highway,
Dad. Up the highway, to DRAMARAMA
CAMP!!! Squeeee!!!!"

**Passing a field full of sheep.
I love sheep! Cute little
fluffy woolly sheep, like sort
of sweaters on legs!**

Guess what, Diary, I have seen cows and
sheep (lots of sheep) and lots of field-things
with no houses on them for miles and miles

and miles. Bill says it is called The Countryside. I have never really been to the countryside before, because when I was living with Mother I always went to places in London which were very nearby, or else to places like Bermuda which were very far away and you just fly over the countryside to get there. And there are no cows and sheep in Bermuda – at any rate not in the resorts that Mother likes to stay at.

Five minutes later.

I wish I could have a drink of water, but we've finished the bottle. Maybe I will finish the Gooey Gums instead, and read some of my book: *Bathsheba and the Affair of the Mysterious Stylist*. It's the new book – it's only just out but it's already on the best-seller list! I am so proud of Mother. In this one, Bathsheba goes on a modeling shoot in

Austria – she is a part-time supermodel as well as everything else – but the stylist on the shoot wants to take over the world and destroy the universe and stuff and Bathsheba has to put her high heels aside and stop him. I am at a really exciting part when she is trapped in a dungeon and the castle is in flames around her, but she manages to escape because she feels a cold draft coming from a wall which turns out to be a secret passage...

Ooh, I have just seen a sign telling us to turn off the highway toward Ozeby! That's the closest town to Dramarama camp! Not long now, dear Diary!

A little later. ♡　✳

Hmm, we think we might have taken a wrong turn somewhere. Anyway, it doesn't matter. It's 3 p.m. now and we don't have to be at

Dramarama camp until 5 p.m. That's lots of time.

Ooh, there is a sheep in the road! Hello, cute little fluffy baa lamb!

Two minutes later.

Ooh, there are lots of sheep in the road. A whole pride of them. Or is that lions?

Three minutes later.

The sheep are not moving.

Four minutes later.

We are not moving either.

Five minutes later.

Bill has been tooting the horn for ages and the sheep are just looking at us and not moving!

    I never noticed before but actually sheep have pretty scary faces when you look at them up close. Sort of cold...and unforgiving.

One minute later.

Bill says it is no problem, we will just find another way around. He says what a good idea it was of his to leave early. His idea! Huh!

    Anyway, tra la, we have lots of time. I'm so glad! I would hate to be late for Dramarama camp.

Ten minutes later.

This   not   road   it
    is   a   exactly
is   of   bumpy
   more   a   track

Two minutes later.

Oh no, dear Diary. We have found
another way around but there are sheep
here too.

Several minutes later.

I HATE sheep!!!
     They have surrounded the car and they
are staring in at us menacingly. Bill is
honking the horn and revving the engine

and it isn't making any difference, they are just mocking us sheepishly!

Oh, dear Diary, will we EVER escape?

What if this is my last diary entry ever? What if I get devoured by sheep and never even get to go to Dramarama camp?

✳

Half an hour later, on a real road, thank heavens!

♡

We were rescued by a farmer, hooray! He came over and chased all the sheep away and showed us another way around our other way around.

But now we're REALLY late. It's 5:15 p.m. already, and I can't see Thespia Hall anywhere... Oh, wait!

Dear Diary, there it is!

Up on the hill, in the middle of the countryside! Dramarama camp, I HAVE ARRIVED!!!

The bathroom
Dramarama camp!!
The world

Dear Keisha,
I'm here. I'm finally at Dramarama camp!
Thespia Hall is just like you said it was
— a gorgeous old castle-y house with
a creaky main staircase made of wood.
The theater isn't actually built into it
but it is built right behind and joined on
by a short corridor. So we won't get wet
going over there if it rains. Oh, of course
you know all this because you were here

last year! I'm just so excited!

So much has happened already, but I don't have time to write it down, because — guess what — I got here LATE, and everyone else is already eating dinner in the cafeteria! I know, I know — HOW could I be late on my first day at Dramarama camp? I completely failed to make a swishingly starry entrance. It wasn't my fault, it was because of sheep. Anyway, I have lots to tell you, about Anita and <u>the</u> Max Singh who is her dad, and his sky-blue sports car and what he said, but not now because Sarah, one of the Assistants, is knocking on the door and asking me if I'm all right and am I ready to go downstairs and have dinner. So, this letter is TO BE CONTINUED...

Not that much later in time, but much, much later in things that have happened...

My dorm! (DORM!!)
Dramarama camp
The world

Hello again, Keisha!
Wow! I can't believe how busy I have been and I've only been here an hour and a half! I haven't even had time to write in my diary — but it is more important to write to you. Anyway, I'm going to copy out my letters and stick them in my diary so they are like diary entries. Ooh, so reading this is like you reading my secret diary, Keisha! You should feel very honored. But don't think that it means you can read my diary all the rest of the time, though. (Ha ha, joke!) (Although you can't.)

So, WHERE do I start?! I know, I will tell you about the other person in my dorm, or at any rate about her luggage, which is all I have seen of her so far. I am NOT in one of the big dorms, but in the smallest possible dorm, with only two beds, right next to the Assistants' rooms – huh! It's because I was late, and there wasn't any space left in the big dorms. Well, there was one bed left in Heather Dorm but they gave that to Anita.

Oh dear, I can see I had better start from the beginning or it will get confusing.

Well, so me and Bill were driving up the really narrow lane that leads to Thespia Hall, and I was really excited and also worried about being late, when all of a sudden this sky-blue sports car drove RIGHT up behind us and started honking its horn! Just as if it was trying to barge its way past. Only it couldn't because there was no space. Bill said some not nice things about it, but it wouldn't go away or stop honking, and as soon as we got into the driveway of Thespia Hall it went VROOOM and surged past us, like a very fast young dog scampering past a slow old dog, and did a screechy stop with flying gravel outside the hall.

"Good grief!" said Bill. "I hope that's not one of your tutors, Bath."

I did wonder if it could be the Dramarama Director, because it was such a fancy car, but it wasn't. We parked right behind the sports car, and just as I got out, this really, really glamorous man got out of the driver's seat. He had the most superstarry sunglasses I have ever seen!

And then a pretty girl our age got out of the other side. She had long brown hair, and

she was wearing this AMAZING bright pink
salwar kameez — you know, like Muneera
in our grade sometimes wears for parties.
She had this wonderful golden scarf to
go with it, and the salwar kameez was all
embroidered with peacock feathers, and I
am almost sure she had real gold earrings.
Really, Keisha, I have never seen anyone
more Princesscular in my life! I wished I
had worn my best tutu instead of my jeans.

Bill got my suitcase out, just as an
Assistant came down the stairs to meet
us all. She was a really nice-looking girl
with short blond hair. She smiled at us and
said, "Hi, my name's Sarah! Which one's
Bathsheba and which is Anita?"

I was just going to say I was me and it
was okay to call me Bath if she wanted,
and sorry I was late, when the glamorous
man said in a very loud, booming voice,

"Just a moment, young lady. I have a word to say to my daughter." And he waved her off as if he was chasing a fly.

Sarah stared, and so did me and Bill. The girl in pink looked REALLY embarrassed. Her dad gave her a big kiss on each cheek and said, "Remember, Anita, you are not just here to have fun! Dramarama camp is for people with serious ambition! You make sure you get the spotlight!"

Anita muttered "Oh, Da-aaa-ad..."

"Now, no nonsense. Nice guys finish last! You stand up for yourself — get a good part where you can really show your talent. Chin up and let me see that megawatt smile!"

Anita did smile, but she looked pretty fed up about it. The man gave a sort of big acting sob.

"Farewell, my daughter," he said. "Think of me sometimes!"

And then he got in his car and drove away with a whoosh of gravel!

The girl looked at Sarah, and said, "Uh... sorry about my father..."

"Oh, never mind," said Sarah, but you could tell she did mind really. "So, I'm guessing you're Anita?"

The girl nodded.

"And that's your father...Max Singh? The Max Singh? Interesting."

I was dying to know why she said "the" and "interesting" like that, Keisha! But I couldn't ask, of course. I didn't even have time. Because the next thing Sarah said was, "Hurry and say goodbye to your father, Bathsheba. Everyone else is already eating dinner in the cafeteria – we'll just get your bags dropped off and then you two can join them."

I skipped up and down with excitement.

But then I noticed that Bill was looking really upset, and I felt guilty. I gave him a big hug. "I'll miss you!" I told him.

"I'll miss you too. Just relax, have fun, enjoy yourself! You're going to have a fantastic time."

His voice was cheerful, but his hug wasn't. I almost felt as if I didn't want to stay after all. But I didn't have time to change my mind, because the minute he let go of me, Sarah just took charge of both of us — me and Anita — and whisked us off into the Hall with our luggage! And that's when I discovered that I was going to be in this tiny dorm called Laurel Dorm, with only one other person, and I started writing to you!

Oh, and dear Keisha, THAT'S what I started the letter with, of course. The other person in my dorm!

Well, I haven't met her yet. I might have

seen her at dinner, but that was all so confused and loud and full of so many people chattering and laughing and knife-and-forking that I can hardly remember anything about it at all, except that Anita had a vegetarian meal and hers looked better than mine so I asked if I could have one too, and I could. Anyway, all through dinner (when I wasn't chatting with Anita, who is really friendly, not like her dad!) I was looking around and wondering who my roommate was, because she has the most quacko luggage I have ever seen in my life. On her bed, there is:

1) One suitcase, which is BLACK.

2) One backpack, which is BLACK, and has silver CHAINS dangling off it.

3) One GUITAR CASE, which is BLACK, and has a SKULL AND CROSSBONES painted on it.

Dear Keisha, how SCARYLICIOUS!!!

I know it's got to be a girl, because of course the boys and the girls all have separate dorms (hooray! No smelly socks).

Maybe she will be a pirate? With an eyepatch and a parrot. Or maybe she will be a vampire? Ooh, maybe the guitar case is really a coffin and she sleeps in it!

Oh, no. I just had a closer look and I don't think she could fit, unless she's very small.

And of course she must LOVE acting just as much as I do because she's here, at Dramarama camp.

Maybe she is a MINIATURE PIRATICAL VAMPIRE ACTRESS!!!!

Oh, wait—

I can hear voices on the stairs! Sarah and someone else...a girl.

Dear Keisha, I think it's my mysterious roommate! I've got to go.

Love and hugs,

Bath xxx

8 p.m. Bedtime in an hour...

Dear Diary,

My roommate is HORRIBLE!

I feel like opening up Keisha's letter to tell her – but I won't. It would only make her feel worried.

If only I'd gotten here a little earlier, I could have been in Heather Dorm with Anita and the older girls and NOT stuck with just one other, unfriendly person! I can't believe I have to share a room with her for two whole weeks!

To be honest, dear Diary, I thought right from the start when she walked in with Sarah that she looked bad-tempered. She was wearing all black, and she had long straight black hair that she sort of draped around her face like a cloak. And when I did get to see her face, I couldn't even tell if she was pretty like Keisha and Anita or just sort of ordinary like me, because she was scowling so much!

But I know you shouldn't judge people by their appearance, so I gave her a BIG smile and said, "Hi! I'm Bathsheba, your roommate! Nice to meet you!"

Dear Diary, she just gave me this look of TOTAL ANGER and said, "Oh, great."

But NOT as if she meant it.

I felt the smile drop off my face.

"Hey! That's not very nice," said Sarah.

"Well, I thought I wasn't going to have a roommate," she said grumpily. "I like being alone."

"Some company will be good for you," said Sarah. "Might teach you some manners." She checked her watch. "I'm going to leave you two to unpack now. You know where I am – just down the hall, past the bathroom. Lights off at 9 p.m. sharp, though. You'll need a good night's sleep before all the hard work starts tomorrow."

"Oh, Sarah, do you know what the theme is this year?" I asked eagerly.

"That'd be telling!" Sarah said mysteriously. "Mrs. Howard will explain everything tomorrow, in her introductory speech."

All the time me and Sarah were talking, my roommate (I still don't know her name) was unpacking her things. And then she sat on her bed and got her guitar out and started doing things to the strings. As soon as Sarah had gone, she started strumming on it. She totally ignored me.

"Wow!" I said. "You're really good." She

is, dear Diary. I could actually recognize the tune, which is not always the case when people play the guitar.

She made a sort of scowly, snarly noise. I am not pretending I was not hurt, dear Diary. I was hurt! A lot!

But I thought I ought to keep trying. Because it is good to be friendly.

"I've always dreamed of coming to Dramarama camp!" I said. "I'm sooo excited about meeting Mrs. Howard tomorrow. I bet she's super gorgeous. Hey, everyone is sooo nice here, aren't they? I think Sarah is great! And I met this really sweet girl named Anita – she came all the way from India and she's ridden on an elephant, how cool is that? She's done lots of modeling and she's even been on a yogurt commercial on Indian TV. But she says it wasn't much fun because the yogurt went bad because it got too hot and she still had to pretend it tasted delicious. Wow, these two weeks are going to be fantastic! I can't wait till week two when the cameras and the Mystery Guest Star arrive."

I sort of trailed off there, dear Diary. I mean, if I'd been having this conversation with practically any of my friends at school, by now they would have said something, like "Me too!" or "Yogurt? Wow!" but this girl hadn't said *anything*. She'd just stopped playing her guitar and was sort of scowling at me in a way that made me suddenly a little worried that actually she really was a piratical vampire.

"Huh!" she said, really scornfully. "Don't be so stupid! Dramarama camp is going to be a total waste. Summer camps always are total wastes. I should know – I've been to tons of them. I practically don't do anything when school is out besides go to summer camps."

"But it's all about acting," I said. "We'll get to act all day, and get *filmed*, and—"

"I hate acting! I'm terrible at it and I hate

everyone staring at me. And I really, really, *really* hate being filmed. And now there's going to be a whole week of it – ugh!"

"Well…why did you come then?"

"Oh, huh, because my dad said that I needed to develop my social skills." She shrugged angrily and turned away.

"Um," I said. I thought I had better not say, *Well, he was right!* "But…but you had to do a whole application form. I mean, they wouldn't have let you in if you weren't good at acting."

She gave a Hollow Laugh.

"Oh, I don't have to worry about that. My father's famous. He can get me into any summer camp in the world."

Dear Diary, that just made me really ANNOYED. She was being so grumpy and now show-offy as well. And I always have to try really hard NOT to be show-offy about my mother, who is actually famous too. And also, I would never use my mother being famous to get things I wanted! (Well, only small things like advance copies of new books in a series I really REALLY want to read. But not for anything big and unfair like Dramarama camp.) And this girl just didn't seem to care.

"Well!" I said. "Actually, I think you should be ashamed of yourself, being so rude and show-offy, especially when I'm just trying to be nice and actually I feel really homesick—"

She looked pretty shocked. "I didn't mean it in a show-offy way—"

I wanted to say more, dear Diary. But I had to stop, because I didn't realize until I had said it that in fact it was true. I DID feel homesick. All I could think was *I miss Bill* and *I miss Keisha* and *I miss Mother* and *This is not what I thought everything would be like!*

"I'm going to write in my diary!" I sobbed. And flopped onto my bed with my back to the HORRIBLE girl and started writing in you, dear Diary. I am so glad you are here at least.

She hasn't said anything for ages.

I keep hearing the guitar sort of starting on songs but they don't get very far before breaking down.

She is very good at the guitar, I have to admit.

Ooh, dear Diary.

I think I heard her mutter "Sorry."

After lights out.

Dear Diary! I just had to write down what happened. I am not miserable anymore. I have made up with Trillian – yes, that's my roommate's name. And if you're thinking that name sounds familiar, well, DD, you're right!

This is what happened after she said "Sorry."

She came over and sat on the corner of my

bed, and patted my shoulder gently.

"I *am* sorry, okay," she said when I turned over. "You're right, I was really rude. I didn't mean to be. It's just…I didn't want to come here! I never get to be at home. I'm always at boarding school, and that isn't much fun, or else at camp. I've been to music camp and sports camp already this summer. I'm just fed up. I want to go home!"

Her voice really wobbled when she said that. I sat up, and, dear Diary, I couldn't be upset with her when I saw how sad she looked.

"Why don't you, then?" I asked.

"There isn't anyone at home. My dad's on tour – he's in Canada now."

"On *tour*?"

She sighed. "Promise you won't tell anyone. But my dad's a rock star. Izzy Wiggin."

I frowned. "That name sounds familiar," I said. "But I don't know who he is."

"It's mainly old people who've heard of him. Anyway, I just wish I could go home, that's all."

"Can't you go and stay with your mother?"

"She's dead."

"Oh," I said. "Oh, I'm really sorry."

"It's okay. I mean, she died years and years ago. I don't really remember her." She shrugged.

Dear Diary, there are shrugs that are just shrugs, and there are shrugs that mean, *I don't want to talk about it because I might cry.* I could tell Trillian's was the second one, and I couldn't help thinking of Keisha. Her dad died just a few years ago, and she remembers him really well and she talks about him and has photos of him and stuff. I wondered if it would be worse, remembering your dead father or mother, or not remembering them, and it made me feel really sad, and sorry for them both. I wanted to give her a hug, but I

wasn't sure she would like it. So I just tried to
look how I was feeling.

"I really wasn't showing off about my dad,"
she said. "I hate that he's famous. I hate that
he's always being on tour. I hate that we
can't go anywhere or do anything without
paparazzi following us around." She sniffed.
"I hate being the center of attention."

DD, I sat right up and stared really hard
at her as if she was an alien, because I cannot
IMAGINE ever feeling like that!

I can't WAIT until I am a famous Movie
Star, and paparazzi follow me everywhere!

I LOVE being the center of attention!
Actually, if I am completely honest, I would
happily be the center of attention forever
and always.

She was so different from me that I
suddenly thought, *Maybe this girl is the
anti-Bathsheba!*

"What's your name?" I asked a bit panic-stricken, because what if it was Abehshtab, which would be Bathsheba backward and that would mean she definitely WAS the anti-Bathsheba.

"Trillian," she said. "I know it's weird."

Dear Diary, there are only so many people with the quacko name of Trillian in the world. And even less of them with famous rock-star fathers! I thought about Keisha's godmother, Natasha, who used to be my housekeeper...

"Do you have a housekeeper named Natasha?" I asked.

Her mouth went all O and she said, "How do you know that?"

Dear Diary, we had such an exciting conversation after that!

It turns out, in fact, that my old housekeeper Natasha now works for Trillian's father. And so this was the very Trillian that Natasha had talked about. Well, there really can't be many people named that, or who

have two brothers named Han and Skywalker.
(The thing was, I'd never heard the name Izzy
Wiggin before because Natasha never calls
Trillian's dad that. She calls him by his real
name, which is Tarquin. Izzy Wiggin is his
stage name.)

So then we talked and talked about what
an amazing coincidence it was, and how nice
Natasha is, and how miserable it is having
parents who are always busy working.

I told her my real name, because it only
seemed fair after she told me about her dad
(although compared to Trillian's dad, Mother
is not famous at all, hardly!) and she said
she had read some Bathsheba books! (I don't
think she was really into them, dear Diary,
she said she likes horror books better, but
she was nice about them.) We were having
such a good time that we didn't think about
unpacking, or even getting changed and
brushing teeth and things like that, until

Sarah came in to turn the lights out, and then we were really surprised at the time and we had to rush to get ready for bed.

And now I am lying here writing in you thanks to the flashlight I cleverly remembered to bring, and chatting with Trillian, my new friend, as well!

Oops, one of the Assistants has just banged on the wall and called, "I can hear you, girls! Time to get your beauty sleep!"

12:00 on my alarm clock...

Dear Diary,
It is midnight!

And I have been woken up by spooky noises!

In London there are always cars going along or people shouting in the distance so you know you are not alone. Here it is really dark and deathly quiet...except for these noises.

Hooo... Ooooo... It sounds just like a ghost in the wall!

Ooh...I wish I had not thought that.

It *could* be a ghost. Thespia Hall is really old, after all.

I tried whispering loudly to Trillian but she is totally asleep. Midnight is a really spooky time. I won't feel safe until it changes to one minute past midnight at least!

Ooh, what if it NEVER changes! What if I am stuck in a Ghostly Time Warp...

Oh, it changed.

Well, anyway, I'll never be able to go back to slee

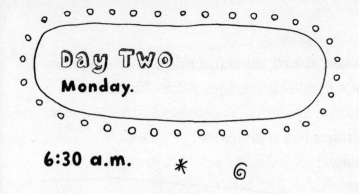

Day Two
Monday.

6:30 a.m.

Yawn... Where am I?

6:32 a.m.

Ooh!

I am at DRAMARAMA CAMP!!! And there is a mysterious, sparkly green envelope lying on my desk! I can see my name written on it in big letters!

6:35 a.m.

I jumped out of bed and got the envelope and

am back in bed, all warm and toasty. I wonder what's inside? It feels just like Christmas!

DD, there is a note inside!
   It says:

WELCOME TO DRAMARAMA CAMP!
TODAY, YOU'RE LOST IN THE
ENCHANTED FOREST, WHERE
THE KING AND QUEEN OF THE
FAIRIES HOLD COURT. WATCH
OUT...YOU MIGHT FALL IN LOVE
OR FIND YOUR HEAD SWITCHED
WITH A DONKEY'S. IT'S MAGIC
THAT RULES HERE!

This must be something to do with the theme. It must be something about magic, and a forest...and a king and queen, and fairies – it must be a fairy-tale theme! Oh, I hope we get to wear beautiful costumes. I'd love to act a good fairy, or maybe a wicked witch. But what about the donkey's head? That sounds a little worrying.

I wonder if Trillian has an envelope too? Just going to look... Ooh, yes, she does, it is on her desk, but hers is blue. I'm dying to see if her note says the same thing as mine, but of course I can't open it.

Hooray, Trillian has just yawned and opened an eye. Back later, dear Diary! Going to find out what's in her envelope!

The tail end of breakfast — writing this among the crumbs.

DD, it's all *sooo* exciting! Everyone has an envelope – one of three different colors: green like me, blue like Trillian, or red. Anita has a green one like me! Each color has a different note inside – like a different story. Trillian's blue one says:

WELCOME TO DRAMARAMA CAMP!
TODAY, YOU HAVE BEEN
SHIPWRECKED ON AN ISLAND. BUT
NOT JUST ANY ISLAND. THIS ISLAND
BELONGS TO AN ENCHANTER.
IT'S FULL OF MAGIC AND SPIRITS.
NOTHING IS AS IT SEEMS…

"What's in the red envelope, what's in the red envelope?" I asked, excitedly.

"Here, you can borrow mine." The boy sitting across from me – I think his name is Charlie – passed me his envelope.

WELCOME TO DRAMARAMA CAMP!
TODAY, YOU FIND YOURSELF
CAUGHT UP IN TRAGEDY AND
INJUSTICE. EVERYTHING SEEMS
TO BE GOING WRONG – AND
THEN, MAGICALLY, THE TRUTH IS
REVEALED. IT'S A HAPPY ENDING.

Everyone is talking about the envelopes and passing them around and wondering what it's all about. Some people say that they're sure it's going to be all about magic tricks and circus acts, but I said I didn't think so because magic tricks aren't acting. But this older girl who was sitting near us said, "It's all performance skills, dear. You wouldn't understand – you're not a real professional." She tossed her shiny brown hair.

Huh! I said, "My drama teacher says I'm very professional!" but no one heard me because they were all busy talking about the envelopes again. Well, no one except Anita and Trillian, who I was sitting next to.

Anita whispered, "That girl's in Heather Dorm with me. Her name's Isabel."

"Well, she's not very nice!" I whispered back.

"Last night in the dorm she kept asking people if they went to a stage school. And she said that if you didn't then you weren't a real professional and shouldn't be here."

"What?!" I squeaked. "How does that work?

Dramarama camp is supposed to be about giving new people a chance!"

Anita shrugged. Trillian said, "Huh. I knew it wouldn't be long before it got cliquey," and stuck her spoon into her grapefruit so a little squirted out and hit Isabel in her eye. Ha.

Anyway, I've got to go now – there's a big meeting with Mrs. Howard in the theater and we all have to go over there!

Dear Keisha,
I am writing this secretly halfway through
Mrs. Howard's welcome speech. She has
just told us that our theme for the camp is
Shakespeare!!!

NOOOOOOO!!!!

Hours of boredom and death. UGH.

We all have to study not one, not two,
but THREE Shakespeare plays. YUCK. And
on the last Saturday evening, we have to
put on a Shakespeare Showcase!

A showcase is like a cabaret. It means
that we don't have to learn a whole part,
but we can choose our favorite scenes
or speeches out of the plays we work on

to perform. We can be in up to three different scenes. But we aren't allowed to do the same speech as someone else, because the audience would get bored. We'll all do a little of everything — acting, stagehand, and set design and everything else.

Mrs. Howard said: "The stories in the envelopes are the stories of the three plays we'll work on — <u>A Midsummer Night's Dream</u>, <u>The Tempest</u> and <u>A Winter's Tale</u>. We thought colored envelopes were a fun way to divide you into groups, and tell you the stories as well. Over the next three days we'll study scenes from the plays in groups, according to the color of envelope you received — so all the reds work on one play, all the greens on another, and the blues on a third. Then we'll trade around, so everyone will have a day studying each of the three plays. After that, you'll be able to sign up for the speeches and scenes you're interested in. If there are clashes, the Assistants and I will sort them out — but we hope to keep rivalry to a minimum. Three plays should give you lots to choose from!"

Oh, Keisha, I don't WANT to do three Shakespeare plays! He's sooooo boring.

The only good thing is that we are going to have a trip to the Playhouse Theater over the weekend, to see a play. Everyone is really excited about it. I haven't been to a real theater in ages! I just hope it isn't more Shakespeare...

Oops, Sarah the Assistant is looking in my direction and frowning. I'd better go, dear Keisha! TO BE CONTINUED...

Lunchtime — I haven't had a single minute to write in my diary all morning! Far too busy with workshops and other exciting things!

Dear Keisha,
Well! Sooo much has happened! First of all, Shakespeare isn't that bad at all. Not the way we're doing it, anyway.

We started the day with a Storytelling Session with an Assistant named Josh. He told us the story of A <u>Midsummer Night's Dream</u>. There are a boy and a girl who are in love, but they have to run away because their parents don't approve and are very upset and angry with them (a little like you and Rafiq). Their friends follow them, but then they all end up falling in love with the wrong people because of magic. That part is okay, but the parts I <u>really</u> like are about the fairies, because they are so magical and glamorous. <u>Their</u> story is that Titania, who's the queen of the fairies, has this little boy who she's adopted, but her husband, Oberon, wants to look after him instead. Titania won't let him take the boy away, and so Oberon's friend Puck casts a mischievous spell on her so she falls in love with the first person she sees. And she falls in love with this man named Bottom who has magically been made to have a donkey's head. (Not a donkey's bottom! That was pretty confusing.) But everything ends happily.

After Josh had explained the story, we did a read-through of Key Scenes. Josh asked us questions about the characters, like how did we think they felt, and how could we show their emotions if we were acting? Then we stopped the reading and tried out some improvisation — you know, acting games and things — and Josh helped us and gave us advice.

Keisha, everyone here is so good at acting! I can see I am going to have to work really hard to get noticed by the <u>Dramarama Diaries</u> cameras. I feel a little worried when I think about it. I wish you were here to talk to!

I think you would like Anita. She lent me her copy of <u>Young Fame!</u>, which is a special Indian edition with Bollywood stars in it. Oh — and I was just flipping through it when I came across the poster in the middle, and guess who it was of? <u>The</u> Max Singh, her dad! She blushed really red when I showed her, and said, "Oh, I forgot that was in there! I wish you hadn't seen it."

"Why? It's really cool – your dad's a famous actor in Bollywood!"

"Yeah, but he's so pushy sometimes. He likes me to get dressed up all the time – like yesterday, I wanted to wear my ordinary clothes but he said I should wear my A-list clothes and jewelry to make an impression." She made a face.

I looked at the bracelet she was wearing. It was gorgeous, Keisha – smooth heavy jade.

"Oh, this one's different," she said. "It's my lucky charm – my granny gave it to me. I love it." She stroked it protectively.

Well, she has definitely made an impression on me, Keisha! Actually...she is almost a little too impressive. Oh, I don't know what I mean by that – only she's <u>sooo</u>

pretty and <u>sooo</u> good at acting, and I sort of think if she was more ordinary she would be even easier to like.

Anyway, my favorite thing today was the Creativity Workshop we did after the Storytelling Session, with Mrs. Howard.

Mrs. Howard is exactly as you described her, Keisha.

Today, she was wearing a long, red robe like a magician — Anita says this is called a kaftan — and her lovely long, black hair went swish-swish-swish as she walked, and smelled of cinnamon.

And I noticed that she has a spooky power, which is when she walks into the room, even when she hasn't been announced, somehow you just know someone important is in the room and you have to be quiet and listen to her. (Trillian says that is called Stage Presence.)

And when she finished her speech this morning, she didn't say "Goodbye and thank you" like a normal person at all! She said, "Farewell! Till we meet again," and then there was a BANG and a flash of light and everyone jumped and squealed, and when we could see again, she had disappeared!!!

Sarah the Assistant says it was stage machinery that did it, and that we might get to try it ourselves sometime this week!

Anyway, I think Mrs. Howard is MAGNIFICACIOUS and I wish she taught at our school!

Everyone was a little in awe of her when she came in to do the workshop, but she made lots of jokes, and got us all organized really quickly so we could play some acting games. One of them was called Musical Statues. We had to move around the room to music, and when the music stopped,

Mrs. Howard called out a person's name, like "Bathsheba!" and a Scene Starter, like "You're a carpenter, lost in a forest!" And then you IMMEDIATELY had to turn yourself into a carpenter lost in a forest, inside your head, and then you had to improv it!

Keisha, as I bet you can imagine, I have NO idea what a carpenter lost in a forest would act like. But I knew I had to do something, so I just quickly pretended to be an old man, and then I thought I would have a sore thumb because of hitting it with a hammer a lot (this happens to Bill whenever he tries to fix things) and then I thought, Ooh, carpenter – forest – woods! So I went around pretending all the other people were trees, and poking them and saying, "Hmm, this one would make a nice door," and things like that, to make them giggle. And you only have to do it for a minute, so it doesn't matter if you only have one idea. Apparently

it's to encourage us to think on our feet
and not be afraid to try things out.

Then we moved on to improvising in
pairs. I worked with Anita, and we had
such fun. I showed her how to Swan — you
know, my Princess Walk where you stick
your nose in the air and sort of drift along
floatily. Mrs. Howard said we were both
good and we really moved scenes forward.
I don't know what that means but it sounds
good!

I must go now, dear Keisha! I've got to
run and get my lunch so I can snag a seat
next to Trillian and Anita. But I WISH you
were here! I like my new friends — but it's
not the same as if you were here too.

Love from B. C. de T.

PS I forgot to even ask about your
granny! Please write to me very soon and
tell me how she is and how you are too...

PPS After lunch we're going to watch a movie of <u>A Midsummer Night's Dream!</u>

PPPS Oh, and you'll never guess what — Anita had a copy of <u>Hail, Bathsheba</u> in her bag, in Hindi. I couldn't help it, I know I am supposed to be incognito, but we get along so well, and after all, I know about her dad. I leaned over and whispered, "Don't tell anyone, but my mother wrote that!" So now I've blown my cover to TWO people — Anita and Trillian — but I think I can trust them.

PPPPS I am opening this letter to write that Trillian's group had a tour of the stage and they found out how to do the flash-bang-disappear trick that Mrs. Howard did, and maybe we'll be able to do it in the showcase! I BET <u>Dramarama Diaries</u> would film that!

After dinner.

Dear Diary,

Trillian is arranging her things on her desk. She has a framed photo of her and her dad and her two brothers, Han and Skywalker. I wish I had remembered to bring photos of Bill and Mother and Keisha. I do miss them – even though I'm having fun. I did get a text from Mother this morning though – that was nice. She said the movie was going really well.

I was just thinking about some things. Like about what Max Singh said. He told Anita that she wasn't here to have fun. He said it was serious work. And that "Nice guys finish last." I know Bill told me to have fun and relax, but actually, I think Max Singh is right. Even though he is rather a rude man. Dramarama camp is my big chance, dear Diary. So I have to be professional. Right?

Professional actresses have to be really

competitive, everyone says so! And fight tooth and nail for their parts!

Hmm...

As you may be able to tell, dear Diary, I have something on my mind.

The thing is, I've found the perfect speech for the showcase. A speech where I not only get to be the center of attention, but act all Princesscular, and Swan, and Swish, just what I am good at!

The trouble is...someone else thinks it's perfect too.

Anita.

You see, this afternoon we watched the *A Midsummer Night's Dream* movie – and it was magical! Everyone was good: Oberon was really handsome, Puck was played by an old man with a sort of mischievous twinkle in his eye, and the humans were really funny with the way they all got mixed up about who they were supposed to be in love with. But the

BEST was Titania. She was just so Queenly and majestic. I kept thinking of Connie Clyde, who got talent-spotted acting Titania...

After the movie, we had to choose a speech we liked from the play, and prepare it. The Assistants helped us with the hard words, and explained everything we needed to know. I spent ages trying to decide on my favorite of Titania's speeches, but I finally decided on the perfect one. It has such beautiful lines and it's really emotional. I wanted to do it just right!

At the end of the workshop, we got to perform our speeches in front of the group. It didn't matter if we didn't remember all the lines – we were allowed the book if we wanted.

I remembered to pause (not rattle it all off very quickly), and to act with my whole body (not just stand there like a log but move around a little). And when I got to a sad line, "But she, being mortal, of that boy did die,"

I did this great Wobble in my voice as if I was Overcome By Emotion. It took me *ages* to get that just right, Diary, and I was so proud of it!

I got loads of applause, and Mrs. Howard smiled at me and said, "Very nicely expressed, Bathsheba." I felt all warm and glowing.

And then it was Anita's turn.

I noticed she was playing with her jade bracelet. She does that when she's nervous.

"What speech are you going to do, Anita?" asked Mrs. Howard.

"Um, the same one as Bath," said Anita. "Is that okay?"

I wasn't sure it *was* okay. But I gave her a big supportive smile anyway.

"That will be interesting – we'll see how differently you interpret it," said Mrs. Howard.

Anita walked into the middle of the room. She just stood there until everyone was quiet, and then started speaking.

Dear Diary, she was really, really, really good. She was Queenly.

I could just imagine her giving orders to servants.

She moves almost as gracefully as Mrs. Howard.

You know what, dear Diary, I think she moves and speaks completely differently when she's in India. I never thought of that before. I mean, if you sometimes wear a sari to exclusive parties then you probably do have to move completely differently than if you wear jeans, or even a tutu. More...majestically. So she is probably completely used to behaving as if she was a queen.

She certainly looked like it, anyway.

And then she did this Pause, just before the sad line, "But she, being mortal, of that boy did die," – and, dear Diary, her Pause was so much better than my Wobble. You could just tell what she was *thinking*. Or, what she would be thinking, if she really was Titania.

There was a *loooong* silence when she got to the end. And then Mrs. Howard said softly, "Very good work." That was all – but you know what, dear Diary? She had tears in her eyes.

She didn't have tears in her eyes when I finished my speech.

Dear Diary, I clapped with everyone else, but inside I felt as if a Tornado had hit me.

After the workshop, before dinner, I went up to Anita and said, "You were really good!" I don't know why, but my voice was sort of not real, even though I really did mean it.

"Thanks!" she said. She gave me a smile, and shyly twisted her jade bracelet around her wrist.

"Um. Were you thinking of being Titania in the showcase? I mean, there's lots of time to decide, I just wondered—"

Anita looked startled.

"Well, yes, I was actually. I've got this great sari I could wear. It would be cool to play her as Indian – I think the Royal Shakespeare Company did something like that—"

"Oh! It's just...I was thinking of being Titania, too."

"Well, you could! Titania has lots of speeches."

"Um. Which speech were *you* thinking of doing?" I asked, hoping and HOPING that she would not say, "The one I just did."

"This one, the one I just did. If I start practicing it now, I think I can get it really good for the showcase."

"Oh!"

I bit my lip. Anita looked at me anxiously. My heart was pounding, dear Diary.

"Um. I did think of doing that speech first," I said, feeling HORRIBLE even as I was saying it.

Before she could answer, a whole bunch of people came pushing past us, going, "Dinnertime, dinnertime, baked ziti, yum yum!" and we had to go off to dinner, and that was the end of the conversation, DD.

But this time, at dinner, I didn't sit with Anita. I went to a different table. Her table filled up really quickly and to be honest I didn't try very hard to sit near her anyway. I could hear everyone telling her how good her speech had been.

When Trillian came in, I saw her do a kind of double take before she came to sit with me.

"Why aren't we sitting with Anita?" she asked.

"We don't always have to sit with the same people," I said, in a very grown-up way.

"Um," said Trillian, and took a big forkful of her baked ziti and looked worried.

Actually, the people we did end up sitting with were not very nice! It was Isabel and her friends. They kept sort of huffing at us as if they wanted us to go away.

"I really think they should keep the kids away from the serious actors," said Isabel, looking right at us. "I think it's awful that the Mystery Guest Star has to be bothered spending her time on coaching amateurs who haven't even been to stage school—"

Trillian carefully knocked her drink into Isabel's lap, and while she was making a fuss, we switched to another table.

Anyway, I am lying here feeling upset with Anita and miserable with everything. I think it is really mean of her to decide to do that speech – after all, I did perform it first. There are lots of others she can do, and I bet she would be better at all of them than me, so why would she care anyway? And she's already been in a yogurt commercial and she ought to let other people have a chance. And I *owe* it to Keisha to get talent-spotted. She said she wanted to see me on the cover of Young Fame!

Except I also feel angry with myself. Huh, crud.

I wish I could bring tears to Mrs. Howard's eyes with *my* amazing acting.

Later.

I told Trillian about the problem. She was reading a book with a werewolf on the cover, but she put it down and listened to me.

"Well?" I said. "What do you think?"

She looked a little shifty. "Do you really want to know what I think?"

"Of course!"

"Well, Bath, I think she's got just as much right to the speech as you do. If you won't give it up, I don't see why she should."

Huh!!!

"Well, Trillian," I said, "that is all very well. But show business is competitive. And you've got to be professional if you want to get noticed. And that means fighting for the good parts! Nice guys finish last! So Anita had just better watch out, that's all! I am NOT going to give up the speech."

"Bath! You wouldn't do anything horrible, would you?"

"No!" I said, really shocked that she'd even have thought that. "I'm just not going to give in, that's all."

Later, later. * ⑥

Huh, what a thing to think. As if I would do anything horrible! I'm not that kind of person.

Even later.

Trillian says she really doesn't want to act in the showcase. She wants to be a stagehand, but Mrs. Howard said she has to try one acting part.

She would be really good at being a stagehand. She says she learned how to move things quickly on and off stage from her dad's roadies. They are the people who carry the drums and things onstage for a big rock band. They used to let her carry the drumsticks.

Still later.

I have been trying out my Wobble in different places.

"Of that boy did *die*."

"Of that *boy* did die."

Like that.

The middle of the night.

Dear Diary!! There are spooky noises going on again! But this time it's scratching noises, and Trillian can hear them too! They're coming from the wall behind her bed.

Trillian woke me up to tell me about them. We are both sitting on my bed with the flashlight, holding hands and being very scared.

Trillian said maybe it's a werewolf like in her book?

I said I didn't think so because werewolves don't scratch, they howl. I said I thought maybe it was a ghost of someone who was bricked up in the wall hundreds of years ago and now is trying to get out.

Trillian says she is not going back to her own bed now I have said that. She is going to sleep head to toe with me. (She says she has washed her feet.)

I am glad; I don't want to be alone either!

I know I won't get any sleep at all tonight!

o o o o o o o o o

Day Three
Tuesday.

6:30 a.m.

Gwwwff... Why is there a foot in my face?

7:00 a.m.

I have a text from Keisha!

I'm really nervous about opening it. What if it's bad news about her granny?

7:20 a.m.

Keisha's granny is much better! She had an

operation, and she still has to stay in the hospital for awhile, but she's out of danger.

Hmm.

I was going to text Keisha right back, and say HOORAY, and tell her everything that's been going on here. But then I just thought, hang on, the main thing that has been going on is me being upset with Anita.

I'm not sure if Keisha would understand the Anita problem. Oh, I mean, she would understand, but I just have this awful feeling that she would tell me that I ought to let Anita have the speech.

Huh.

7:50 a.m.

Dear Diary,

I have started lots of letters to Keisha. And crossed them out again. It would be awfully annoying if she wrote back and told me to give the speech to Anita.

Keisha is great, but I don't know if she would understand about Titania maybe being the Part I Was Born To Play. Sometimes she can be awfully grown-up and say things like "There are other parts."

And I don't think she would understand at all about Max Singh and his "Nice guys finish last!" idea.

Huh, now I think of it, Keisha is a Nice Guy (or Girl) and she finishes first all the time, like in the hundred meters race on sports day. She's good at everything, including being nice. Not like me.

Sometimes being nice doesn't feel easy at all.

Maybe I will just not write to Keisha. Not right

now, anyway. At least I know her granny is okay. That is the important thing.

Maybe Anita will change her mind about the part.

8 a.m. At breakfast. ☆ ✳

Crud. On the way down I saw Anita in her dorm, trying on a sari. She looked amazingly Queenly. And she was muttering words under her breath. I recognized those words. I have been practicing them too.

She was trying out her Pause in different places:

"Of that boy...did die."
"...Of that boy did die."
"Of that boy did...die."

I wish I had a sari.

Morning break. We always have doughnuts for morning break — yum yum!

Our group is doing *The Tempest* today. There's a princess named Miranda – only she doesn't know she's a princess – who's been shipwrecked on an island with her father Prospero for years and years. But Prospero is secretly a powerful magician, and has lots of servants who are spirits, like fairies, who work for him. There's a pretty spirit named Ariel, and a scary one named Caliban. Ariel has some nice songs.

But there isn't a speech as good as Titania's.

Lunchtime.

Well, that was a weird workshop we just had.

I'm not sure if it went well – or really badly!

Mrs. Howard picked me to pretend to
be Prospero, the powerful magician, and
someone else played one of my spirit servants.
The servant had to act out an emotion – like
happiness, or sadness, or pity – and I had
to guess which emotion it was and mimic it.
As soon as I guessed, someone else came up
to replace the servant. It was a really quick,
energetic game, and it was all going fine until
Anita ran up as the servant!

We goggled at each other, not knowing
what to say. Suddenly – I think it was because
I was so worked up because I was acting – all
I could think about was wanting to be Titania.
And I think she was thinking the same thing.
There was dead silence while everyone
stared at us, and I desperately tried to think
of something to start the dialogue with that
wasn't about Titania!

I haven't had stage fright for ages, but

suddenly I couldn't think of a thing to say. Anita frowned at the floor and twisted her bracelet around. In the end I just stomped off and sat down. I felt as if I was going to cry.

I don't care if Mrs. Howard's angry, I thought. *I can't do it!*

But the next thing I heard was lots and lots of clapping, and Mrs. Howard saying excitedly, "Brilliant! Simply brilliant, girls – why, you really persuaded us you were angry with each other! And not a word of speech needed, you did that all through miming!"

I blinked in astonishment.

Mrs. Howard strode up and down enthusiastically.

"This is what I'm talking about when I tell you to move a scene *forward!*" she told us. "See how Bathsheba reacted instinctively, and how Anita really forced her to feel that emotion? That's one of the hardest parts of acting. Fantastic, girls. You two will go far!"

Go far! Wow!

I glanced at Anita. She gave me a small smile. Suddenly I just wanted to giggle. We smiled at each other awkwardly, and then we laughed.

I might try and talk to Anita later on, about the Titania speech. Maybe things will be okay after all. I think I will call Bill, and tell him how well things are going...

Just before dinner.

Dear Diary,
I tried to talk to Anita – and it was horrible!

I finally gathered all my courage and went downstairs and knocked on the door of Heather Dorm. Anita was inside, sitting on her bed.

"Bath!" she said, jumping up. A sheet of paper fell off her lap. I glanced at it briefly.

Just long enough to realize it was Titania's lines.

"I just came to say hello," I said, feeling bad because of course I hadn't.

"Oh!" said Anita. "Hi!" She cast a guilty glance toward her sheet of lines.

I sat on her bed and we chatted about who we thought the Mystery Guest Star would be, but it was a little awkward. I just couldn't think how to bring up the subject of the speech.

"Wasn't it amazing what Mrs. Howard said about us?" she said. "I'm still glowing!"

"Yes! It's so encouraging. I am going to work so hard to get in front of the *Dramarama Diaries* cameras!" I sighed. "I can't wait for week two when they get here. It's as if the real excitement hasn't even begun yet!"

"I know!" said Anita. "But it's so important to be really prepared before they get here. We've got to make the most of week one as well."

Okay, I thought. *Now or never.*

I took a deep breath. "I see you're learning Titania's speech," I said.

Anita folded her arms. "Yes. I am."

"I really want to do that speech, Anita," I said.

"Well, so do I!"

"There are loads of other speeches!"

"So do one of them, then!"

She glared at me. I glared at her.

"I think you're being really mean," I said.

"Why? It's not *your* speech!"

"I saw it first!"

"No you didn't!"

Dear Diary, I suppose there must have been some good way to end this conversation, but I couldn't think of one. And then I realized that we'd been speaking a bit louder than we'd meant to, and Isabel and all the other girls from the dorm were looking at us as if we were nuts. So I stomped out.

How did it turn out this way? I feel really hurt and upset.

Later.

At dinner, Trillian said, "There are loads of other speeches you could do, Bath! You can take part in up to three scenes or speeches, as long as you can remember them, that's what the Assistants said. Hey, you could even have mine and do six, if you want!"

(I do feel a little tempted to do six, but I bet I would never be able to remember them all. It's important to be focused, like Connie Clyde said.)

And anyway, I want to do just *one* speech – the one I know I can do really well – the show-stopping one – the perfect speech!

And of that boy *did die.*

My Wobble deserves to be in the showcase.

I've got to do something about this awful situation.

I know. I'll go and ask Mrs. Howard what to do!

Back in my dorm. ♡ ☆

Okay, dear Diary, that was NOT what I expected to happen at all!

I went down to the entrance hall and to Mrs. Howard's office.

I knocked on the door.

"Come in," said Mrs. Howard from behind it.

I went in – and, dear Diary, I stopped short. Because there stood Anita! She looked really startled to see me.

"Bathsheba," said Mrs. Howard. "What can I do for you?"

"Um...I...um...I'll come back later," I said, or rather, stuttered.

"Why? Because Anita's here?"

I didn't know what to say.

"I suppose that you have come to see me for the same reason as Anita. She was just telling me about it. I am used to dealing with clashes like these – at any stage school you have to expect it. But I'm sorry to see you two in conflict."

I didn't look at Anita. I felt all crunched up inside. I hadn't considered that she would be as upset as me, and want to talk to Mrs. Howard too. I wondered what she had been saying about me. I wondered guiltily if I'd done anything mean. But I hadn't. Just thought mean thoughts, which isn't the same, although it made me feel just as guilty.

"Why don't you tell me your side of the story, Bath?" said Mrs. Howard. "Let's see if we can find a solution."

"Well," I said, "well, the trouble is...me and Anita both want to do the same speech."

I stopped there. Because, dear Diary, I couldn't say I had a right to the speech, because I knew I didn't. And I couldn't say Anita had done anything mean, because she hadn't.

"Ah," said Mrs. Howard. "That is exactly what Anita said too. I'm glad you agree on the problem, at least." There was a small smile in her voice as she said that. "Now let's see if we can't come to some arrangement. Isn't there some other character you might like to get into? Ariel? Miranda?"

We shook our heads.

"Titania does have more than one speech, you know."

"But I want to do that one," we both said together. I glared at Anita and she glared back at me.

Mrs. Howard sighed.

"So I can't ask either of you to be reasonable, and generous, and give up the speech for the other's sake? You were getting along so well, both of you, and acting so well together. It seems a shame to spoil that wonderful stage chemistry."

I steeled myself, DD. *I can't just give in and be nice,* I told myself. *I can't be weak! What about my Big Chance? What about the cover of* Young Fame!

Anita shook her head firmly.

"You see," I said, in a small squeak of a voice, "I was *born* to play Titania! And it has to be this speech. It's perfect."

Mrs. Howard shook her head sadly.

"Very well. The solution is quite simple – you'll have to audition for the speech."

"Audition?" said Anita, and, *Audition?* I thought.

"Yes, of course. Did you think you were the only two people who ever wanted to do the same speech?" She pulled out a big schedule from her desk, with AUDITIONS written on it in red ink. "There's a third girl who's mentioned she's interested in the same speech, believe it or not."

"What?" we said in chorus.

"Yes. Isabel, from your dorm, Anita." She wrote down our names in the book. "I prefer to spend as little time as possible on auditions since we have only two weeks, and this camp is all about learning to work well with different people. That includes being mature enough to come to an agreement about who does which speech. But we always have some people who won't compromise, and so I've decided to hold auditions on Thursday morning. I'm sure you can get ready by then, can't you?"

"Thursday? But that's...that's in two days' time!" I said. I hastily ran over the speech in my mind. I didn't know it perfectly. Not even half perfectly!

"Can we have time off from the other workshops?" asked Anita.

"No, I'm afraid not. Dramarama is all about hard work, you know that very well. You'll have to fit your preparation into your spare time. If you're dedicated enough, I'm sure you'll find a way."

I snuck a glance at Anita. She looked just as shocked as me.

I didn't know what to say to Anita when we were out in the hall together, dear Diary.

I didn't feel at all happy, although an audition is perfectly fair. I just hope I'm good enough by Thursday.

I don't think Anita knew what to say to me either.

I could have said "I'm sorry you're upset," or "Break a leg" (which is actor-speak for "Good luck"), or "I'm not trying to be mean." I thought of saying all those things. But by the time I looked toward her, she was already heading to her dorm.

When I got back to Laurel Dorm, Trillian was playing her guitar quietly and singing along. I realized it was one of the songs from the musical of *The Tempest* that we'd seen earlier.

"Wow, Trillian, that's really good!" I exclaimed, forgetting about my own problems for a moment. "You should perform that in the showcase."

"Ugh, no way!" Trillian dropped her guitar on the bed and made a face. "Everyone would say I was just trying to be like Dad."

I think she still doesn't like it here. Poor Trillian! The only thing she's enthusiastic about is the doughnuts we get at break. (They *are* very nice. Sometimes with sugar sprinkles.) But she is very kindly helping me learn my lines by prompting me. Destiny and Determination! I WILL get the part!

o   o   o   o   o   o   o   O   o

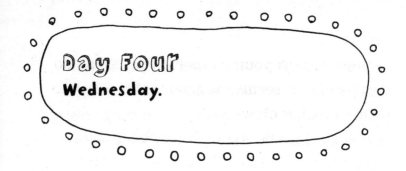

Day Four
Wednesday.

Today my group is doing the third play
– which is called *A Winter's Tale* – and we're
doing a workshop with a stuntman in the
afternoon!

He is named Miles Fearless, and he has
been in seventeen car crashes and has jumped
out of many exploding helicopters and fallen
off twenty-nine tall buildings. Also he is set on
fire once a day on average.

It is astonishing he is still alive, but of
course he does all of it very safely, and that is
what he is here to teach us. Not jumping out
of helicopters and things, thank heavens –
more like how to act sword-fighting, and how
to fall. Falling is apparently very important,

as you can hurt yourself badly if you don't do it correctly. (It seems the safest thing is not to do it at all, but oh well.)

It is going to be so much fun, but I don't think I'll be able to really concentrate and enjoy it because of trying to memorize my speech for Titania. It is running around and around my head.

Ugh, I wish I could have the whole day off. Maybe no one would notice if I skipped the morning Storytelling Session and went up to the dorm to work on my speech...

Mid-morning break. ☆ Doughnuts again — the jammy kind this time! ♭

Huh! I got caught sneaking off, by Josh, and he made me go to the *Winter's Tale* Storytelling Session after all. I think A

Winter's Tale isn't as interesting as the other two plays – there aren't any fairies or spirits. Oh, and there's a Queen who gets turned into a statue right at the beginning and not turned back till the end – that's one part I definitely don't want to play!

Afternoon break.

Ooh, Miles Fearless is really cool. And he taught us how to do all kinds of exciting things like fall backward and not hurt yourself. We had to fall into each other's arms, to show how important it is to be able to trust your partner, and how important it is to CONCENTRATE. And later on, he's going to teach us how to do the flash-bang-disappear trick!!

It would be great – if I wasn't so worried about finding time to rehearse my speech!

After dinner.

No time to rehearse. We had our first meeting
to plan the showcase in the cafeteria after
dinner. It was the first time we could sign up
for the speeches and scenes we wanted to do.
But when the sheet got passed around, I saw
that Mrs. Howard had already written *Titania*
and the line numbers of the speech next to my
name, and Anita's, and Isabel's.

Mrs. Howard led the meeting, but all of us
got to say our ideas for the showcase. It turns
out that lots of people want to do the same
speeches, and the audition schedule got
passed around too. Charlie and his friends
are going to do a sword-fighting scene from
A Winter's Tale, and a comedy scene from
A Midsummer Night's Dream.

Charlie is really nice. He even said that I
could be in their comedy scene if I wanted.
I would have to say: "O dainty duck! O dear!"

Yes, really. Shakespeare is *quacko*.

I said: "No thank you, Charlie. I am going to be Titania."

I only noticed after I'd said it that Anita was sitting really close to me. She didn't say anything. I hope she didn't think I was being horrible. But I AM going to be Titania. I'm determined!

Mrs. Howard frowned when she heard I was just going for that one part.

"Bath, why put all your eggs in one basket? Why don't you join in one of the other scenes, or learn another of Titania's speeches?"

She doesn't understand, dear Diary. I have my costume all planned in my head. I could see exactly the things I was going to use when we did a tour of the Wardrobe department last night. It will be made of net curtains, all white and floaty, and I will put tinsel in it so I glitter, and it will be just the most Princesscular thing ever...

You know when you just have a funny feeling about something? Well, I have a funny feeling that I WILL get the part. I'm sure of it! It's DESTINY, just like Connie Clyde said in Young Fame!....

Oh, and – big surprise! – Trillian signed up really enthusiastically to play the statue-fied Queen in *A Winter's Tale*!

I said, "But why, Trillian, why? She gets turned into a statue. She doesn't do anything!"

"Ha ha, exactly," said Trillian, with Devilish Glee. "I won't have to act! I will just wrap a sheet around me, and dunk myself in flour, and ta-dah, I will be a statue! And I'll stand totally still, and not do anything for the whole time I am onstage, which I bet won't be very long, because Mrs. Howard will see how boring it is and tell me to leave! Hooray!"

DD, she is the most quacko girl ever.

It is a good idea for a costume, though.

Later.

Dear Diary, something weird and awful has happened!

I was rehearsing my Titania speech, with Trillian prompting me, when we heard someone running up the stairs sounding all upset and out of breath. We looked at each other and stopped rehearsing, and then someone knocked wildly on the door.

"Come in?" said Trillian.

It was Anita.

She looked...I don't know...distraught. She gave me a quick glance. Dear Diary, she looked so angry and *suspicious*. I wondered what on earth I'd done wrong. I was going to say hello, but that look just made the word sort of dry up on my tongue!

Then she turned her back on me.

"Have you seen my bracelet?" she asked Trillian.

I looked at her arm. Sure enough, her jade bracelet wasn't there.

"I put it on my dressing table when I went for a shower, and it wasn't there when I came back." She did that gulp that means you're about to cry.

"Maybe it just fell down the back?" I asked.

She gave a big sob and ignored me. Trillian jumped up and put an arm around her. I wanted to as well, but somehow I didn't dare to.

"My granny gave it to me," Anita sobbed. "It's my lucky charm – I've never passed an audition without wearing it!"

"Come on," said Trillian, "We'll go and ask the Assistants. I'll come with you..." She glanced at me worriedly.

Dear Diary, I didn't know what to say. I wanted to offer to go and help as well, but the way Anita was behaving, it didn't seem as if she wanted my help!

"Thanks," Anita sobbed to Trillian.

They went out the door.

"Um, I'll stay here then," I said quietly.

I have been trying to rehearse by myself, but I can't really concentrate, dear Diary.

I feel so guilty.

I ought to be helping Anita look for her bracelet.

But it really didn't seem as if she wanted me to.

I'm scared that if I go after her now and offer to help, she'll snap at me and say something awful. Why did she look at me like that? It was HORRIBLE. I can't forget it. I feel really hurt.

Later.   * β

Trillian is back.

They didn't find the bracelet.

Trillian keeps looking at me as if she wants to say something, but then she doesn't.

In bed. Lights off. But I keep tossing and turning...

I keep having these horrible dreams where I'm Titania and I'm really upset because I've lost my bracelet, and Keisha won't comfort me, she's just glad I've lost it. And then a ghost comes out of the wall and goes, "Ooo, I am going to get yooo, for not helping Anita... wooo..."

And the words from my speech go around and around my head...and around and around...

o   o   o   o   o   o   o   o   o

Day Five
Thursday.

7:57 a.m.

Oh no, dear Diary! I overslept!! And it's the audition for Titania today!

I'm supposed to be at the theater early, so I have just half an hour to get washed, dressed, eat breakfast and get there!

10:30 a.m — after the audition.

DD, I am never going to oversleep again.

You won't believe the trouble it's caused!

What happened was, I leaped out of bed as soon as I realized I was late, and rushed to the shower. But there was someone in it. I banged and banged on the door but they didn't stop the water.

Trillian poked her head out of the dorm, still looking a bit bleary (she overslept too – oops!), and said, "You'd better go downstairs and use their shower, quick, Bath!"

So I had to RUN downstairs with my washbag to the next floor – which is where Anita's dorm is. I barged past all the older girls who were getting ready to go down to breakfast, saying, "Sorry, sorry," and rushed into their bathroom instead. As soon as I'd finished in the shower I looked at the time. There was no way I'd have time for breakfast. I decided to just brush my teeth and go straight to the audition. So I squirted out some toothpaste and got brushing.

"Oh yuck!" I'd dropped my toothbrush right down the back of the sink where all the fluff and dust was. I bent down to pick it up.

And that's when I saw it. Only I didn't realize what it was.

I noticed that the floorboard my toothbrush was lying on was loose, and a corner of it had chipped off. There was a kind of flash of green underneath it, down with all the dust.

"Huh?" I said. I thought about lifting up the board to see what it was. But then I remembered I was LATE LATE LATE. I grabbed my toothbrush and flung the door open, foaming at the mouth, dear Diary, because I hadn't had time to rinse, and I rushed out and down to my audition.

I ran down the stairs and along to the theater. There stood Mrs. Howard at the door, waiting for me.

"I'm so sorry!" I gasped, nearly in tears as

I skidded up to her. "I overslept!"

"Well, come on – you're holding everyone up." She steered me through the backstage entrance.

"Now take a moment to collect yourself," she said as we came out onto the stage, behind the curtains, "and I'll call you when it's time. Why are you carrying your toothbrush?"

I looked down at my hand. Sure enough, I was still clutching my toothbrush.

"It's a...um...a prop," I said wildly.

(WHY did I say that, dear Diary? WHY??)

"Really?" Mrs. Howard brightened up. "How original! Well, I can't wait to see your interpretation. Titania, Queen of the Tooth Fairies and her magical toothbrush, perhaps? Wonderful!"

And she just glided off majestically between the curtains, leaving me staring at the toothbrush with not one single idea in my head of how I was going to work it into my speech, dear Diary.

I took some deep breaths.

"Well...uh...um...you can be my magic wand," I told the toothbrush.

The toothbrush didn't look convinced.

"We're ready for you now, Bathsheba," Mrs. Howard called from behind the curtain.

This was it. I took deep breaths, but, Diary, I felt sick. I'd been rushing so much that I'd rushed every line of my speech out of my head. I had no idea how my speech went. I didn't even know what it was about! All I could think about was my toothbrush—

"Bathsheba?" Mrs. Howard sounded irritated.

"Coming," I whimpered.

I stepped through the curtain. I blinked in the light. Mrs. Howard was sitting in the third row, with a pen poised over a notebook. There was another person sitting just behind her – Isabel, the girl from Anita's dorm who went to a stage school. She looked relaxed and confident, as if she did auditions all the time – which, of course, she did. Being from a stage school.

I gritted my teeth. *I'll show her,* I thought. And – just like that – my first lines popped back into my head. I raised the toothbrush with a Queenly gesture.

"The fairy land buys not the child of me..." I began, and suddenly I remembered *all* my speech, Diary!

And it might even have gone really well. Except...

...Just before I got to the line "Of that boy did die," I saw the door at the back of the theater open, silently. And in came another figure, dressed in a sari. Anita!

She sat down quietly in the back row, but I could see, even from this distance, that she was absolutely miserable. It was something about her shoulders.

I hesitated. Suddenly I couldn't remember where I had decided to put the Wobble in "Of that boy did die." I gazed at my toothbrush for inspiration. And that's when it hit me.

Toothbrush – Anita.

Anita – toothbrush.

The green glint that I'd seen under the floorboard when I'd dropped this very toothbrush – it had to be Anita's bracelet! Nothing else was that exact shade of green!

Mrs. Howard cleared her throat.

"Of that boy did die!" I gasped, completely forgetting the Wobble.

Dear Diary, the rest of the speech is a blur. I couldn't stop thinking about Anita's bracelet. *What was it* doing *down there?* My mouth tied itself in knots. I forgot words, and there were awful pauses. And – in those pauses – I slowly and horribly realized that Mrs. Howard was laughing. Yes – LAUGHING. I could see her shoulders shaking.

It was like one of those nightmares when the whole school sees your underwear or something.

I came to the end of the speech and didn't even bother finishing up with a grand gesture or anything. The only good thing I could think of was that now, finally, I could tell Anita where her bracelet was. At any rate, dear Diary, even if I'd miserably failed my audition, I knew I would still like Anita to have the speech more than Isabel. I opened my mouth to tell her...

And then Mrs. Howard started clapping!

"What an excellent idea to play Titania as a wholly comic character, Bathsheba! I don't think it's ever been attempted before, and yet you pulled it off! Extraordinary! Well done!" She wiped tears from her eyes. Tears of laughter.

I just stood there opening and shutting my mouth. A *comic* character?

Mrs. Howard pointed behind me, toward the curtain.

"Go out that way, if you don't mind."

"But…" I said. I tried to catch Anita's eye, but she was too far back and she was staring at the floor anyway.

"But nothing. Off you go. Anita? You're up next."

Anita got up and started making her way down to the front. Her anklets jingled as she went. I tried to make meaningful faces so she would understand I had something to tell her, but she didn't even look at me!

"*Off*, Bath!" said Mrs. Howard. "Hurry up – we're already running late because of you."

I retreated behind the curtain, because, dear Diary, when Mrs. Howard says *Off* like that, you off. Anyway, I had just had a great idea. I would rush up to the bathroom, get the bracelet out from under the floorboard, and rush down here and come in through the back of the theater and wave the bracelet so Anita would see it and know it was safe. But I knew I'd have to run!

A very dramatic couple of hours later...

Except it wasn't quite that simple. The bathroom had a *Closed for cleaning* sign hung on it.

"It's a matter of life and death!" I howled through the keyhole.

Finally, finally the door opened and the cleaner came grumpily out with her cart. I dashed in and slammed the door. Then I went past the bathroom stalls and under the sink. I used the end of my toothbrush to lever up the loose floorboard. And there it lay – the jade bracelet. It was covered in yuck, but it wasn't broken or anything. I wondered if I still had time to get it down to the theater—

And then someone rushed, jingling, through the door, banged into one of the bathroom stalls, and started sobbing.

I got up and went back to the stalls. I listened at the door. Then I bent down and looked under it.

"Anita?" I said to the anklets.

More sobbing.

"Anita? Are you okay?"

There was a pause, and then a tear-choked voice.

"I don't even care that Mrs. Howard says you get the speech! Or that Isabel forgot all her words. I really don't care. But my bracelet! My granny gave it to me, and I miss her *sooo* much, and she's so far away, and I want to go home..."

I bent down and pushed the bracelet under the door. It lay there glinting and green. I straightened up. *I got the speech!* I thought, but I didn't feel happy about it.

There was more sniffing, and then silence.

And then the stall door whipped open.

There stood Anita, her face red with crying, holding her bracelet and looking totally shocked. I was a little surprised that she didn't look *happy*, dear Diary. I thought I would have made everything better by finding it for her. But she was looking at me...strangely. *Well, I thought, I don't blame her! I should have told her before.*

"I saw it this morning," I said quickly. "But I didn't realize." I explained everything.

Anita gazed at me suspiciously. I felt a little hurt, dear Diary. I wasn't expecting her to exactly hug me (especially as my hands were really dirty still from being on the floor) but I did think she might have said thank you.

"So...you really didn't hide it yourself so I'd be upset and make a mess of my audition?" she said.

I opened my mouth BIG with shock.

"No!!"

Dear Diary, I hadn't even thought that she might think that! And yet...suddenly I could see how she might. I hadn't helped her look for it. And I hadn't wanted her to do well in the audition. I hadn't even told her "break a leg."

I took a deep breath. I wanted to convince her that I wasn't her rival, but her friend. Suddenly that mattered a lot more to me than having the speech. She was so nice, and I didn't want her to be upset.

"There's only one person who should have that speech," I said. "I didn't mean to play it as a comic part. And I don't want to – it's your part. Come on. Let's go and ask Mrs. Howard if you can have it instead."

Anita looked at me as if she couldn't believe her eyes.

"You mean...you're giving up the speech? For me?"

"The audition wasn't fair," I said. "If you hadn't been so upset you would have done the best." And then I swallowed and said in a big rush so I couldn't take it back, "You play Titania better than I ever could!"

Anita gave me a wobbly smile.

"Thanks. You know, this really, really means a lot to me. And not just because I'd love to play Titania. It's just...my dad wants me to be an actress so much. I was worried I wouldn't find another speech I could do well – I mean, I'm only good at serious roles. And then I'd be a failure and he'd shout, and—" She was crying again.

"Oh dear," I said, "oh dear." I nearly said "O dainty duck," but I managed to stop myself. I stepped into the stall to give her a hug. We were both inside – which I think is why Isabel didn't see us when she came through the door, went straight past us to the sink where I'd found the bracelet, and crouched down near the floorboard. She drew in her breath in a shocked gasp. "Oh no! It's gone—" and then she turned around and saw me and Anita peering around the stall door at her.

She glanced at the bracelet on Anita's wrist, and she blushed really red. Then she glanced at me. I must have looked shocked, because she quickly got up, backed away and ran out of the bathroom.

Anita made a squeaking noise and grabbed my arm. "Did you see her face?!"

"Yes! It was her who hid your bracelet, wasn't it?"

"It must be! She knew it was my lucky charm – she knew how much it meant to me. I told her the first day I got here, before I realized she was horrible."

Anita looked me straight in the face.

"Bath...I...I'm so glad it wasn't you who took it!" she said breathlessly. "I didn't think you would do that. You seemed so nice! But

then…I didn't know what to think. I'm sorry
I didn't believe you right away, but I do
now."

I patted her hand, feeling a little hurt, but
also very relieved that she finally, definitely
believed me.

"That's okay," I said. "Let's go and tell Mrs.
Howard about the speech."

"Do you think we should tell her who we
think took the bracelet too?" Anita asked me.

I thought hard.

"No, I don't think so. I mean, it's our word
against Isabel's, isn't it? And besides, she
only did it to give herself more of a chance in
the audition. I don't think she'll do it again.
Especially not now that she's given herself
away like that!"

"Why are people so mean?" said Anita
miserably as we walked down the stairs to
Mrs. Howard's office. "Sometimes I think all
actors are horrible!"

"No they're not! I'm not, and you're not, and nor is Mrs. Howard or Sarah or Josh, or lots of people… But I know what you mean. You know that actress named Avocado Dieppe?"

"Oh, yes! I watch her TV show all the time. *Avocado Unpeeled*."

Huh!

"Well, *she's* horrible. I met her at my mother's book singing. She was completely rude to my best friend, Keisha, and she's a total show-off and obsessed with her looks. And," I said with a shiver as I remembered, "the worst thing is she's actually playing Bathsheba Clarice de Trop in the movie: *Bathsheba Superstar*." I sighed. "Sometimes I think Mother likes her better than me."

"I'm sure she doesn't," Anita said warmly.

Brr, yuck, I feel all upset when I remember Avocado. Thank heavens she isn't here to spoil everything now!

Much later — just before dinner.

Dear Diary,

Trillian is really happy me and Anita are friends again. She hasn't said anything about it, but I can't help wondering if she thought I might have taken the bracelet, too...

I hate that they might have thought I was the kind of person who would do that.

And I keep thinking, *Could I have done something different, so they wouldn't have ever thought it was me?*

I suppose I could have given up the speech to Anita right away. Then they never would have suspected me.

But how am I supposed to become a great actress if I go around giving up speeches all the time?

Oh it is so confusing, dear Diary.

I still don't even have a speech to do in the

showcase. What am I going to do?

Maybe I will get some ideas and inspiration at the showcase meeting this evening.

Even later — after the meeting. 6 *

Wow, I am really tired! We cram so much into the day, dear Diary – I am much busier than I even normally am at school!

At the meeting, Mrs. Howard told us that nearly everyone had gotten a speech or scene, so tomorrow we could work on our props and costumes, and we would all work on the scenery together. We talked about how we wanted the scenery to be, and Mrs. Howard and the Assistants suggested how to make it look real.

"Nearly everyone" having a speech does not include me, dear Diary.

I can't think of a single speech I'd like.
All the good girls' parts have been taken…
Besides, I want something SPECIAL.

Even horrible Isabel has got a speech.
She muscled in on Charlie's comic scene
and she's going to play Thisbe, who as far
as I understand it is a girl who falls in love
with a wall. Mmm…okaaaay.

But the *Dramarama Diaries* crew will
be here in just a few days, and so will the
Mystery Guest Star and how am I going to get
coached when I don't even have a speech?

Oh, I wonder who the Mystery Guest Star
will be… Maybe it will be someone from a
soap – that would be really cool! I could get
their autograph for my friends at school.
Trillian hopes it will be the presenter from
Spooky Britain but I don't think he counts as
a Star. He is really old.

And my lines for Titania keep going around
my head… Typical! They were so hard to learn

and now I don't need them anymore I can't forget them!

Much, much later.

Dear Diary!
We have found out the source of the ghostly noises!!!

There is a SECRET ROOM in our dorm!

Trillian woke me up because she could hear the ghostly scratchings again. They were coming from right behind her bed, inside the wall.

We shivered and squealed for awhile, but quietly so as not to wake up the Assistants, and then Trillian squeaked and said, "Ooh, I can feel cold air coming from the wall!"

Dear Diary, those were almost exactly the same words that Bathsheba uses in *Bathsheba and the Affair of the Mysterious Stylist*, before she finds the way out of the dungeon!

I jumped up and got the book. I turned the pages quickly.

"I'm sure I read it in here – oh yes, this is it!"

"What are you talking about?"

"Look, it's right here! Bathsheba in the book is trapped in this ancient dungeon. But she feels a cold draft coming from the wall, and she realizes that means there's a passage behind it! So she taps on the wall until it sounds different—"

"—and that means it's hollow!" finished Trillian excitedly.

She started tapping the top of the wood paneling, and I tapped the bottom. All of a sudden it sounded completely different! I started feeling around a little, and, dear Diary, I found a bolt! We hadn't found it before because it was really small and hidden by the bed. I opened it, and then we had to pry the panel open because there wasn't a handle.

We could only get it open a crack because of the bed being close up against it, but as soon as we did, we heard this *HOOOO...WHOOOO...*noise like a ghost, and something went *FLAPPA-CLAPPA-FLAPPA* and I clapped my hand over my mouth so as not to scream. But Trillian bounced up and down on the bed wildly.

"It's owls!" she hissed at me. "Owls! We have them in the barn where Dad keeps his Ferraris!" And then she added, "Ooh! We've found a secret room!"

We didn't get to explore it because we'd have to pull the bed away and we might have woken the Assistants up, but we're going to try tomorrow. I can't wait! Trillian says there must be a window, too, because otherwise how would the owls get in and out?

Maybe Anita would like to come too? Though I'm not sure she's the exploring type. But I would like to show her we really are friends by including her.

Maybe no one has discovered it at all, ever, except us!

Trillian says at least one other person would have discovered it – the person who built the house. Actually they would have built it. Well, we can at least be the first people to discover it since them.

It is still amazing!!!

o   o   o   o   o   o   o   o   o

Day Six
Friday, break time.

We got up really early and pulled the bed out a little. Guess what – it is not just a room, it is a whole passage! We went along it a ways with the flashlight. One way it is all full of owl poop and feathers and it looks as if there's a wall anyway, so we didn't go that way. The other way it goes on for ages! We didn't go very far down, because we didn't have time, but we will explore it more later. I have been making lists of all kinds of things we'll have to take on the expedition, like cookies and flashlights, and a cell phone, and blankets and water, because we don't know how far it will go on for. Trillian says it will be really spooky and maybe we will see a ghost or something.

I'm not sure I want to see a ghost, but exploring sounds fun...

I've been helping Anita with her costume. I had to smother a jealous twinge as I pinned up her flowing skirt, dear Diary. She's bound to get filmed. And I don't even have a speech yet.

Wardrobe Workshop
Dramarama camp
— with owls!
England

Dear Keisha,
I'm so glad your granny is well again! Thank you for texting to tell me. Now you can have ooh-la-la France fun! I am almost jealous, except of course I'm at Dramarama camp and the Mystery Guest Star is going

to arrive sometime this weekend, so I can't be jealous! Ooh, I can't wait to see who it will be! I wonder what it will be like getting coaching from them. I hope they teach me all kinds of Movie Star secrets, like how to make the audience cry, and how to flick your hair impressively.

Today was lots of fun. I spent all morning helping make costumes. I wish I had been making my own costume, but since I don't have a part yet, I can't. Sigh.

My friend Anita is going to be Titania, Queen of the Fairies. It is such a gorgeous part and she does the speech really well. To be honest, Keisha, I was jealous of her to begin with and we argued. But we made up, so never mind. I helped her with her costume. She's going to wear a sari with gold embroidery. She looks so Queenly!

In the afternoon, I helped paint scenery.

I painted a forest, a desert island and a palace. Trillian was there too, and we had a little paint fight, but the Assistant wasn't too angry! These older girls made a big fuss though, just because a TINY drop of white paint got on their stormy night. It didn't spoil it, it just looked like stars. They think they are special just because they go to stage school!

Ooh, and we discovered a secret passage! And lots more has happened, but it is almost time for the showcase meeting so I have to go. Maybe I will think of a good speech to do at the meeting. I don't want to be stuck being a Rude Carpenter or something and have to say, "O dainty duck."

Big hugs,
Bath
PS I hope your granny is getting better and better!

Later.

Dear Diary,

Well, that was an exciting meeting! It finally feels as if the showcase is REALLY going to happen! I mean, I know it was always going to, but now it really does feel real! Everyone showed off the costumes and the scenery that they'd made, and it looks *soooo* cool and professional. Mrs. Howard said, "I'm really proud of you all! You've clearly been hard at work."

Of course, I still don't have a speech. But, on the other hand, I had an amazing idea which is going to make the showcase even better.

When we'd all finished talking about how the scenery was going to go together, and would it all stand up, and could we hang the clouds from the lighting rig or would that end in disaster, and discussing which order people should come on in, and who still hadn't gotten a speech (me), there was a pause while Mrs. Howard frowned at her notes.

"So let me see," she said. "Our running order is: a fairy queen, a real queen turned into a statue, three magicians all doing different speeches, a princess, a man with a donkey's head, followed by lots of songs and dances and people falling in and out of love all over the place. Is it me, or does it seem a little...confusing?"

There was a worried silence.

"I wanted a showcase instead of a play so everyone would have a chance to shine. But it's not working as well as I hoped. We need a rethink. Perhaps more of a storyline?"

"But it's not meant to be a story," said one of the older girls. "It's a showcase – a cabaret."

"It still feels...I don't know, as if it's lacking a thread. Something to pull it all together.

Even showcases can have a theme."

"What about the theme of 'Total Madness'?" suggested Trillian.

Everyone laughed.

"That's a little negative, isn't it?" said Mrs. Howard with a smile. "Some things that happen in Shakespeare might seem, well, surreal, but madness is going a bit far."

"How about calling it *Ye Olde Shakespearean Bouquet*?" suggested another girl. "Like, all the different acts are different flowers in a pretty garden..."

She was drowned out by a wave of groans from the boys, and not just the boys, dear Diary. I could hear Trillian making sick noises.

And that's when I had the idea. Trillian. Statue. Theme!

"I know!" I cried. "We could start the whole show with the Queen – that's Trillian – being turned into a statue – you know, from the first act of *A Winter's Tale*. Maybe that could happen with the house lights still up." I could suddenly see just how it would all work. "And then we could have a voiceover, you know, as she freezes into a statue. It could say something like, *Follow me, fair gentlefolk, into a statue's dream...* And then the house lights could go down, and the footlights could come up, you know, so it all turns dreamlike and magical, and the play begins...and then the showcase acts could begin! And the whole showcase could be a dream that the Queen – Trillian – has when she's turned into a statue. Because all kinds of crazy, surreal things can happen in dreams, can't they? And when all the acts are over, we can do the scene where Trillian gets turned back alive again, and her dream ends."

There was a second's pause, and then Josh grinned widely. "I like that idea!" he said. "The house lights going down, and the voiceover – nice!"

"Me too!"

"Yeah!"

I looked at Mrs. Howard. What would she think of it?

"I think that's an excellent idea," said Mrs. Howard. "And the statue – Trillian – can be onstage throughout." She started making enthusiastic notes. "Yes, the Queen's statue will be the central point, the eternal spectator, if you will..."

"Uh – what?" said Trillian, looking horrified.

"Don't worry, you can rest during the scene changes. But I think you need to be there, visible to the audience. To provide counterpoint to the action. Great idea, Bathsheba! *The Statue's Dream* – how about that for a title?"

Dear Diary, I felt *sooo* proud!

Until Trillian turned to me and muttered angrily: "Thanks a lot, Bath! Now I've got to be onstage for the whole play!"

Oops, dear Diary!

But thankfully she's not furious with me, just annoyed. She says it *is* a good idea, but she just hates everyone looking at her.

She did admit to me later that Dramarama camp wasn't as bad as she thought it would be, though. "I mean, I've made friends," she said. "But I still wish I could go home!"

Poor Trillian. I can understand how she feels. I'm so busy I hardly have time to miss anyone, but I *do* miss Bill, a little. Maybe I'll call him...

Up in my dorm, trying not to feel homesick after my long chat with Bill...

Hmmm...

You know, dear Diary, I feel as if all day I've been being the nice guy.

I helped Anita with her costume (even though it *was* quite heart-wrenching, thinking that it could have been me being Titania).

I painted scenery for everyone else's scenes.

I thought of a good idea to make the showcase even better.

But I still don't have a part of my own!

And now Trillian has disappeared and so has Anita. I suppose they are all busy practicing their lines or something, and aren't thinking about me at all. Well, Anita will be practicing her lines (sigh – *my* lines...). Trillian might be practicing standing still covered in flour, I suppose.

They're not thinking about me.

Maybe nice guys really DO finish last.

Bouncing around, thrilled with excitement!

Dear Diary,

I love my friends!!!

I was just slumping around on my bed feeling sorry for myself when in came Trillian and Anita.

They BOTH gave me big hugs, and then Trillian said, "Okay, Bath, we've decided on a great plan! We're going to have fun, and at the same time—"

"We're going to help you find a part for the showcase!" said Anita. "You've been so fantastic today, helping me with my costume, and coming up with that great idea for *The Statue's Dream* –" Trillian rolled her eyes – "and we can't have you with no part of your own! So tonight –" her voice dropped to a mysterious whisper – "we're going to have a council of war!"

"Ooh!" I said, really excited.

"Well, not of war exactly, more like a council of Find A Good Part For Bath," said Trillian. "We're going to have it in the secret passage so the Assistants can't hear us staying up late—"

"Ooh!"

"And it's going to be at *midnight* and we're going to have a feast too!" said Anita.

"Ooh! Yay, yay, yay!" I bounced up and down on the bed. "I've always wanted a midnight feast – Bathsheba in the books always has them and I never have!"

So that's what we're doing tonight, dear Diary! Anita is going to sneak upstairs after lights out and we're going to get together all the snacks that we have left (not much in my case) and we're going to have a feast and try to find a part for me!

Really late at night — past midnight!

I am writing this in the secret passage, wrapped in a blanket! We've just finished our midnight feast. It was so cool – we had one bag of salt and vinegar potato chips, half a pack of soggy chocolate cookies, and Trillian brought lots of doughnuts left over from morning break. Anita brought this amazing bag of stuff which is like seeds and puffed rice and things all dyed different colors! It smells really nice but not like food. But we ate it anyway – it was gorgeous. Mmm!

We explored the passage too. There are holes in the outside wall, where the owls get in and out. And, most interestingly, there are stairs at the end that go all the way down to the ground. We found a bolted door at the bottom. And a mop leaning against it, so I don't think we are the first ever to discover it after all. Huh! We unbolted the door a little just to see where it went, and it led right outside – it is covered with ivy out there.

Trillian and Anita have been trying to find a part for me. Trillian even said I could be the statue, but I don't want flour in my hair. *Dramarama Diaries* will never film that.

The trouble is, there are just no girls' parts left that are any fun.

I don't want to be an extra fairy or a serving maid or something. It needs to be something spectacular. Hmm, so much for our council of war.

Still later, probably morning.

Me and Trillian are back in bed now. Anita kept falling asleep, so we decided to stop.

Guess what – before we left the secret passage, Anita said she thought the Mystery

Guest Star might be her dad, Max Singh!

"Honestly, it's the kind of thing he'd do," she said miserably.

"Why do you think that?" I asked excitedly.

"Well, he always turns up at my school unexpectedly. He says it's to see me, but I think he likes being mobbed for autographs too. And he kept going on about wanting to broaden his appeal in the UK... I don't know, I just have a hunch! I hope it isn't him though!"

I'm finding it hard to go to sleep now. I keep wondering about the Mystery Guest Star and wondering who it will be. I can't believe that the day after tomorrow (or even tomorrow already!) there's going to be a celebrity here and CAMERAS! And that I'm going to – if I'm lucky – be featured on *Dramarama Diaries*, the UK's most watched talent show!

Trillian says she doesn't want to be filmed at all! She said, "Maybe I'll cut my hair so I look like a boy. They don't film the boys as much."

"No, that's true," I agreed. "It's not really fair..."

"But it means more chances for us of getting filmed!" said Anita. Which is very true.

Ooh, it's going to be *sooo* exciting. And in just a few days we'll be rehearsing the actual showcase. Oh, I *have* to find a good speech soon. I just can't stop thinking about it.

I can't even lie still, let alone go to sleep!

But I'm going to try anyway.

Goodnight, dear Diary! Sweet dreams!

O   O   O   O   O   O   O   O   O

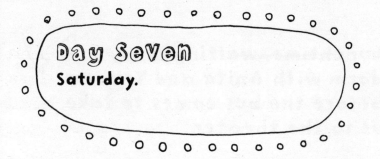

Dear Diary,

Wow, I'm really tired after last night! Good thing that Saturday morning is sort of a rest morning. We get to sleep in an extra hour. I really need it!

But it's not totally a rest morning, because we get to choose between different fun activities – not acting ones but things like Fencing and Archery and Indian Dance. Trillian chose to do Fencing. I chose to do Indian Dance with Anita. Maybe it will help me be more graceful and Queenly like her.

Lunchtime, waiting in my dorm with Anita and Trillian before the bus comes to take us to the theater.

It struck me as we were doing an Indian Dance pose that involved standing on one leg and rolling your eyes, dear Diary, that Dramarama camp is halfway over already!

I was struck with such despair that I lost my balance and fell off my one leg.

Oh, Diary, have I done all the things I meant to at Dramarama camp?

Let me see...here is the list I wrote...

☆ Make a swishingly sashaying starry ENTRANCE arm in arm with Keisha!

Um...nope.

☆ Snag beds right next to each other in one

of the big dorms so we can meet lots of people and make lots of new friends.

I don't have a bed in a big dorm like Anita, but I have met lots of people and made new friends anyway!

☆ Work hard at every single workshop and make the Mystery Guest Star really impressed with our acting talent.

Well, I HAVE been working hard. I hope the Mystery Guest Star will be impressed by me!

☆ GET NOTICED by the cameras from <u>Dramarama Diaries</u>!

That, dear Diary, is my GOAL for next week!

Um, so, my score is one out of four so far (half a point for 2 and half a point for 3). But I still

have a week of Dramarama camp left to go!
Things can only get better.

Oh, someone's knocking at the door.

A few minutes later.

Dear Diary, wow!!
    You'll never guess who was at the door
– Mrs. Howard! And she wants me to compère
the showcase!
    If you're wondering what compèring is,
well so was I. Apparently, the compère is the
person who introduces all the acts.
    SQUEEEE!!!
    When I called "Come in!" I wasn't expecting
it to be Mrs. Howard, at all.
    "Bathsheba, can I talk to you?" she said.
    I nodded, a little overawed. She sat down on
my bed with a swoosh of her hair.

"I was so impressed by the kind way you gave up the Titania part to Anita. And you are such a talented actress yourself, I would hate to see you without a part."

(Mrs. Howard thinks I'm TALENTED!!!! Wow!!!)

"So I wondered if you would like to compère the show?"

"Compare it with what?" I asked, but then she explained, and I was really excited!

It is going to be so cool! I know I'm not actually acting a Shakespearean part, which is a pity, but I come onstage really often. And I get to write my own lines to introduce the acts, and to say goodbye to the audience as well. I am kind of the star of the show!

I am so thrilled! And Anita and Trillian are doubly and triply thrilled for me, too!

Ooh, I just checked out the window and the bus is here! We're off to the Playhouse, dear

Diary! I can't wait to find out what the play will be...

On the bus, sitting next to Trillian.

Isabel and her friends are sitting in front of us. They're going on and on about who they think the Mystery Guest Star will be.

I hope the Mystery Guest Star isn't Max Singh. I don't think I like him all that much, especially not if he shouts at Anita. My dad – Bill – would never shout at me. Not for something silly like not getting a part, anyway.

It's funny how sometimes famous actors and actresses can be really horrible. Like Avocado Dieppe. Yucketty.

Anyway, who cares? I am going to be a COMPÈRE!!!

Still on the bus, feeling a little depressed...

Gosh, seems like I can't get away from Avocado Dieppe. A copy of Young Fame! was being passed around the bus, and there she was, smirking on the front page. Anita really wanted to read the article. Huh!

"I wonder if any of us will ever get as famous as Avocado Dieppe," she said wistfully.

"I wouldn't want to," said Trillian decidedly.

"I would!" I said. "But not if I ended up that mean." I explained to Trillian what happened when I met Avocado with Mother and how show-offy she was.

Hmm, dear Diary, have just been having this lovely daydream about being a famous actress, and everyone loving me because I am so nice, and I will be all humble and say, "But really, I'm not that talented..." when of course I actually will be...

Ooh!

We are here. We are at the Playhouse!

Write in you later, dear Diary – I'm off to see a play!

In the Dramarama bus
A busy road
England

Dear Keisha,

I just had to write to you at once!

You see, Mrs. Howard has asked me to compère the showcase! And that's not all – then I went to see <u>A Midsummer Night's Dream</u> at the Playhouse, and you know what? In THEIR production, Puck was a girl!

"But," you are probably saying, "Puck is a boy's part! And in the movie you saw, he was an old man, a little like a leprechaun!"

Well, yes, but here he was played by a girl, and she – I mean he – just stole the show. The way they acted the play was so different from the movie we saw: much more modern and cool. I realized about halfway through that Puck is just like a compère, too. It's his job to tell the audience everything they need to know, and make sure that the right things happen in the story. And he has the very last speech of the play. He comes on after the curtain has fallen, and says a wonderful, funny, goodbye speech to the audience, all about how he hopes they liked the play, but if they didn't they could just pretend it was a dream.

And I've had such a brainwave! Because

I'm the compère for the showcase, I have to say goodbye to the audience at the end, as well. So, I'm going to learn Puck's final speech and say it at the end as a goodbye. At last, I'll have a speech to act — and it even rhymes!

Oh, the play was so fantastic. I wish you'd been there! For the forest, they just had strings of Christmas lights hanging down from the lighting grid. It sounds as if it would be really bare, but it wasn't, it looked all enchanted, as if it was Christmas or something! It looked <u>sooo</u> much better than our painted trees, and even better than the forest they had on the movie.

Ooh, I've got to stop writing, because the bus ride is so bumpy I can't write well, BUT, I got the autograph of the actress who played Puck! Her name's Adora Bell, and she's <u>sooo</u> gorgeous and <u>sooo</u> nice! She was coming out of the theater at the same time we were. I saw her and sort of <u>squeeeed</u> and pointed and jumped up and down. Anita and Trillian were laughing at how starstruck I was, but in a nice way.

"Oh, I SO want her to sign my program," I wibbled.

"So go and ask her then!" said Anita.

"But what if she says no?!"

"Don't be silly!" said Trillian. And she and Anita each grabbed one of my arms and marched me right up to Adora Bell!

Trillian said, "This is our friend, she's an actress too!" and Anita said, "She'd like your autograph, please!" and I sort of went "Glaaaeeeeoooo-igg-urk!" or something, because I was <u>sooo</u> starstruck.

But Adora Bell was just lovely, and she smiled and signed my program, and then she asked if we'd come with our parents, and we said no, Dramarama camp, and she said: "Really? I went to Dramarama camp when I was a teenager!"

"Did you get spotted by the <u>Dramarama Diaries</u> cameras?" I asked (because I'd recovered my Poise and Grace a little by then).

"No! They didn't exist then." She laughed. "But it didn't stop me from going on to stage school — and look at me now!"

"How did you know Puck was the Part You Were Born to Play?" I asked eagerly.

"I didn't! What do you mean?"

"Well, you know, when no other role will do..."

"I don't think it works like that. I've played lots of different roles — big parts, small parts, everything. I just try to make each one as good as I can. It's all experience!"

Wow, Keisha.

She is <u>sooo</u> inspiring!

Anyway, I really have to go because we're practically back now, and there seems to be something in the lane blocking our way, so I'd better look out and see what's happening.

Lots of love,

Bath

Later — in shock!!!

Dear Diary,

You are NOT going to believe what has happened.

Is it a good thing that has happened? you may be wondering.

Well. How can I put this?

NO.

NO NO NO NO NO NO NO NO.

It is not a good thing.

It is – quite possibly –

DISASTROUS!

The Mystery Guest Star has arrived.

And guess who it is?

Not Max Singh.

Not someone from a soap.

It is…

Oh, I had better start from the beginning.
So you can truly appreciate the entire, total
awfulness of the event that has just RUINED
MY LIFE.

As the bus drove up the lane toward the Hall,
we could see at once that something was going
on. There was a limousine on the road – well,
partly in the hedge. Assistants were hurrying
back and forth, carrying bright-pink and

lime-green luggage. Someone had dropped a bag in the lane and I could see women's clothes lying all over the road.

Me and Anita and Trillian and everyone else craned our necks to see out of the window.

"What do you think the Assistants are *doing*?" Trillian said.

"I think the limo's stuck in a muddy part and they're trying to get all the luggage out of it. Wow, whoever it is has so much stuff!" said Anita.

"They must have come to the wrong place," I said. "No one would bring all that stuff just for one week! Even Mother."

"Sit down, girls!" called Mrs. Howard, so we did, but we still kept leaning over to see. Eventually the limo managed to squeeze itself out of the hedge and backward past the bus, and we drove on into the grounds. Mrs. Howard got out and we all hurried after her, curious to see what was going on.

I grabbed Sarah as she rushed past. "Sarah! What's happening?"

"I don't have time to talk, Bath. There are still things to bring in—" She ran off back toward the limousine.

"Josh!" shouted Trillian as he came toward us, dragging a huge lime-green trunk with gold snakes molded onto the corners. "Who's in the limo? What's going on?"

Josh didn't stop, but as he heaved the trunk up the steps he panted, "Mystery...Guest... Star!"

I shrieked, and Anita jumped up and down. Even Trillian was excited. "No way! She's not supposed to be here until tomorrow!" she said.

"She must have come early! Anyway, how do you know it's a she?" I asked.

"All those skirts and bras, and pink and green luggage?"

"It's not my dad, it's not my dad!" Anita did a happy dance.

"This is *sooo* exciting!" I said. "Let's go and find her. Or at least someone who knows who she is!"

We rushed into the Hall. I saw Mrs. Howard hurrying into her office, talking to a crowd of Assistants who were with her. No one was paying any attention to us – they were all too busy.

I was just going to suggest that we not exactly listen at Mrs. Howard's office door but sort of just stand around near it and hear things, when Sarah came rushing past again, and grabbed Trillian by the shoulder. "Do you have a flat iron?" she demanded.

"Flat iron?" Trillian stared. "No!"

"Oh, rats! She's lost her handbag and it had her flat iron in it as well as Smoochy Woo, and she's kicking up *such* a fuss."

"Who is, who is?" I asked, but Sarah wasn't listening.

"One of the girls in my dorm has a flat iron," said Anita.

"Great! Can you come with me to find her so I can get it and bring it down, please? She's demanding to straighten her hair before she comes out of the office..."

"Who? Who?" we all shouted, but Sarah was already running off up the stairs, dragging Anita behind her.

Me and Trillian looked at each other blankly. Then I noticed something. There was a huge pile of luggage by the door, but there was a handbag (lime green with pink tassels) sitting just by the stairs, slightly hidden by a potted plant.

I nudged Trillian and pointed it out to her.

"Do you think that's the handbag?" I asked her.

"I suppose it must be! I wonder what Smoochy Woo is?"

"Probably a brand of hair gel," I said

absently, because, dear Diary, I had just had what I THOUGHT was a stunning idea!

I would collect the handbag and take it into the office. Thus being nice and helpful and also finding out who the Mystery Guest Star was!

I went over to the handbag and reached out to pick it up. Okay, it was in the shadow of the potted plant – so I couldn't be sure – but I had a funny feeling it moved.

I shook my head. Handbags didn't move! It did smell a little strange. But that was probably just the hair gel or something. Or perfume. Some perfumes do smell weird.

I reached out, and picked up the bag firmly by the strap.

It happened very quickly, dear Diary. Very quickly – and very horribly. You know how if spiders give you a yucky shiver, and then you just happen to adjust your top or something and a spider LOOMS at you from it? It was like that. Except worse.

Because the bag growled! And barked! And tried to bite my hand!

I SHRIEKED and flung the bag up in the air. I didn't mean to! It was just automatic!

"It's ALIVE!" I squealed, as the bag shot up in the air and a whole rainbow of lipstick and jewelry and loose change came flying out. Trillian screamed too, and as the bag fell to the floor and skidded across the room toward Mrs. Howard's office, I just kept wildly thinking that, even if a bag was made of leather and fur and crocodile skin, it still shouldn't actually *growl*!

The bag came to a halt and grew a head. The head of a small, ugly, bad-tempered goblin. At least, that's what it looked like. I blinked and peered closer.

"It's a…a…dog," said Trillian breathlessly.

It was. A dog. A small, almost-hairless, angry-looking dog. It gave off a very weird smell, sort of a cross between a boy's bedroom and school dinners. Also inside the bag was a flat iron, and the dog had its paws on it, as if it was guarding it.

The dog bared its teeth and started barking fiercely. The door of Mrs. Howard's office opened. Someone wearing the brightest yellow minidress, and the highest stilettos, and the glossiest, bounciest, most expensive-looking hair, and the biggest SUPERSTAR sunglasses I'd ever seen in my life came storming out, screaming in an American accent: "Leave my darling Smoochy Woo alone!"

She snatched up the dog in one hand and her flat iron in the other. Then she reached up and with one finger tilted her sunglasses so she could see us better. She looked right at me.

"Oh!" she said, blankly. "It's you!"

Dear Diary, I opened and closed my mouth silently, as you do in a nightmare when you just can't scream no matter how hard you try.

It was Avocado Dieppe.

o　o　o　o　o　o　o　o　o

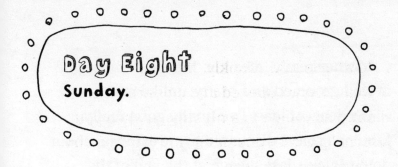

Day Eight
Sunday.

Dear Diary,

Help.

I hardly slept at all. I can't believe Avocado Dieppe is the Mystery Guest Star! And actually sleeping on the same corridor as me – because of course her room is up here with the Assistants and Mrs. Howard.

She didn't say much to me last night – Mrs. Howard hurried her off for official stuff – but I get the impression she is not glad to see me either.

It is weird to think that she has seen Mother more recently than I have, because of shooting the Bathsheba movie in Hollywood with her.

Mother really likes her. Maybe because she is well groomed and pretty, unlike me.

Oh dear. At least I've finally got a really fabulous role. I discussed my great idea, about doing Puck's last speech at the end of the showcase, with Mrs. Howard. She thought it was a good idea and she had an even better one: she said I should compère the whole show in the character of Puck! So I'll have a costume and everything. I'll write my own lines to introduce the acts, and then right at the end, after Trillian gets turned back into the Queen, I'll deliver Puck's final speech. I can't wait – it's going to be so much fun!

And the *Dramarama Diaries* crew is arriving today!!! Maybe things won't be too bad, even though Avocado is here.

Later.

I am just taking a break from making my
costume. (It is going to be gorgeous! A deep
green net skirt, with silk leaves for the bodice,
and a starry hairband.) Anita's been helping
me with it. She's really good at sewing! I want
it to be ready for the first full rehearsal
tomorrow – I can't wait to try out my Puck
character!

Mrs. Howard made a speech to us at
lunch, introducing Avocado. Everyone is
so starstruck! Just because she was in *The
Princess Gang* and stars in a TV series named
after her. Huh, anyone can do that.

Avocado made a speech back. She said,
"Hi! I'm Avocado – well, you recognize me
of course – everyone recognizes me!!!" Yuck,
yuck, yuck. And then she made her dog – he
was sitting on her lap with his paws up on the
table – do a little wave with its paw and said,

"And this is Smoochy Woo! My trusted advisor! I always say to directors, if you want to work with me, you have to talk to Smoochy first."

Everyone went "Awwwww." Huh. I *like* dogs, dear Diary. But this one smells funny. And does not seem very friendly.

I caught his eye as Avocado was finishing her meal. Dear Diary, he GLARED. (I think it is his eyebrows that do it.) And then he growled, and then he started barking! Avocado cooed at him and tried to get him to eat a piece of egg, but he kept on snarling at me.

I shrank back into my chair, wondering what I'd done wrong.

"He can smell your fear," muttered Trillian.

"I'm not *scared*! I just don't like him much!"

"Oh, I think he's *sooo* cute," sighed Anita. "Avocado has such an amazing life!"

Yes, dear Diary. Anita is starstruck!

"I am such a fan of her TV show!" she

gushed as we went out of the cafeteria. "She always looks *sooo* glamorous! I love her Trend Tips For Groovy Chix column in *Starz!* magazine too!" She caught my eye and looked embarrassed. "I mean, if she's as mean as you say, obviously that's awful..."

"What do you mean, *if*?!"

"I don't mean I don't believe you," she said quickly. "It's just that Mrs. Howard praised her so much in her speech..."

That's true, dear Diary. She did. I could hardly tell she was talking about the same person! But of course she mostly talked about her acting, and not her character.

Well, maybe Avocado has changed. Maybe she is not so bad after all.

People like her, after all.

People such as Mother...

Oh, I can't concentrate, dear Diary, there is so much noise going on outside. I'm going to go and tell the people who are running up and down the stairs that SOME people are trying to learn their lines! (In between writing their diary, ahem…)

A moment later.

Ooh!!!!
There is a very good reason for the noise!!!
The *Dramarama Diaries* film crew has arrived!!!!

Later. Feeling very, very, very fed up!

Okay, dear Diary. Forget what I said earlier. Avocado has not changed at all. She is just as bad as ever!
When I heard the cameras had arrived, I rushed down the stairs. Trillian was just

coming out of a workroom with a piece of scenery she was painting.

"Come on, come on!" I pulled her after me.

Outside there was a big, important-looking bus. Men and women were getting out, and unloading lots of exciting equipment, like big cameras, and tripods, and those fluffy microphones that look like dead Persian cats on sticks.

I grabbed Trillian and jumped up and down in excitement.

"It's happening, it's really happening, I'm going to be on *Dramarama Diaries*! Come on – let's go and introduce ourselves."

Trillian pulled away. "Not me! Don't tell them about my dad – please!"

"Of course I won't if you don't want me to!" I said, feeling a little sorry she wasn't pleased about the cameras. "But don't you want to be on TV?"

"NO! I'm going to hide in the dorm. You

have fun..." And she hurried off.

I gazed at the film crew. They were all rushing around looking busy and important and organized, dear Diary. It made me feel like a play does – my heart beat faster and I wanted to be part of it all. Maybe right at the center of it all! Oh, dear Diary...I just dream that one day people will notice me!

Suddenly one of the crew – a tall woman with a big nose – looked up and exclaimed, "Look everyone! It's Bathsheba Clarice de Trop!"

Everyone turned and stared and smiled. I turned pink and then red and then felt a huge smile spread over my face.

"Hi!!!" I said, in my most star-like voice.

The tall woman frowned and shook her head. "Sorry, dear. I meant behind you..." And then someone pushed past me so hard I nearly fell over.

It was Avocado. She was carrying Smoochy Woo. He smirked at me as they went by.

"Hi!!!" she said to the woman.

"But—!!!" I said.

Nobody heard me. Nobody even noticed me.

The woman reached for a camera and focused on her.

"So, Avocado Dieppe, how does it feel to be playing one of the most famous names in children's literature?" she asked Avocado. "Finally Bathsheba makes it to the silver screen – in *Bathsheba Superstar*! How does it feel to be Bathsheba Clarice de Trop?"

Avocado smiled and tossed her hair.

"Well, I'm just, like, so into Bathsheba. We're just...connected. I'm ambitious and a perfectionist, just like her. I live the same glamorous lifestyle. I guess, I'm used to being a winner – just like her!!!"

"But—!!!" I said again.

"We'll have to get an actual interview with you. You don't mind, do you?" said the woman to Avocado.

I just stood there blankly while she fixed Avocado up with a microphone and walked off with her toward the bus, Avocado still going on and on about how she was born to be Bathsheba, and how she understood every emotion that went through her head, and how this was the role she was born to play, and...

"But *I'm* Bathsheba Clarice de Trop!" I whimpered.

No one heard. I was going to run up to the woman and grab her sleeve and tell her who I really was – but then a thought struck me. Like a bolt of lightning.

Nobody at Dramarama camp – except the staff, of course, and Anita and Trillian – knows that I'm really Bathsheba Clarice de Trop. Everyone else thinks I'm Bathsheba Smithee!

So if I suddenly tell the Dramarama Diaries *crew who I am, it'll be a big shock for everyone. They might even think I was trying to get unfair attention from the cameras!*

After all, even Trillian and Anita got the wrong impression about me and the bracelet. I didn't want anyone else getting the wrong idea like that!

But did that mean I had to let Avocado get away with pretending to be me? Even if she wasn't really pretending to be me but pretending to be a character with the same name as me...or not really pretending but acting...

Dear Diary, my head was starting to spin. I heaved a big and confused sigh, turned and went back to the costume workshop.

Evening.

Okay, dear Diary – I'm even MORE confused now!

I was alone in the dorm, learning my lines, when there was a knock on the door.

"Come in," I called.

The door opened and in came the last person I expected to see – Avocado!

I dropped my script.

"Hi," she said. She smiled, but she looked nervous and fidgety. "I just came to, you know, give you a piece of advice!"

Advice???

I stared at her suspiciously.

"About acting?"

"Well, yeah, sort of!" She sat down on my bed – without being asked.

"Look, Bathsheba, Mrs. Howard says you're here anonymously. I just want to say, I think that's really, really cool. I mean, I'm totally only really in Britain to promote the movie, *Bathsheba Superstar*. The *Dramarama Diaries* cameras want to focus on me, obviously –" she flicked her hair – "and I want to talk about the movie. If you were to let slip that you were the so-called *real* Bathsheba, I think that would really not be cool! Like, it would be bad for the movie."

"What do you mean?"

"Well, I understand how you might be tempted to tell the camera crew who you really are. I mean, anything for a little more airtime, right?! But if I were you – I just wouldn't."

"Oh," I said. My heart was beating fast. "Is that a threat?"

"What an idea! It's just that clear publicity is *sooo* important to a movie's success, and we don't want to confuse people." She glanced at me with a bit of a sneer. "I mean, we want to give the impression that Bathsheba is, like, a glamorous, *cool* character. And you don't really fit the message. You're so...uh, gauche. It would really suck if the audience got the wrong idea about the movie because you insisted on telling everyone who you are for selfish reasons. I mean, you want your mother's movie to be a success, don't you?

You don't want to spoil it for her, do you?"

I just didn't know what to say, dear Diary. Gauche? What does gauche mean?

Avocado got up with a final smile. She seemed more confident now.

"Think about it!" she said jauntily. "I'm sure you'll see I'm right."

And she Swanned out.

Dear Diary, I don't know what to think!

Would it really make people not like the movie if I told them I was the real Bathsheba?

I don't want to spoil things for Mother!

And anyway, I'd already *decided* to be anonymous. And that was okay.

But I hate the idea that Avocado thinks she is *making* me be anonymous.

Oh no – I feel all miserable now.

And I wish I knew what gauche meant!

After asking everyone what gauche means.

Sarah says gauche means awkward and clumsy!

Huh! I am NOT awkward and clumsy! On the contrary, Anita says I am quite graceful at Indian Dance.

Later.

Anita was really shocked when I told her what Avocado said to me. Trillian was really angry.

"Huh, how dare she say you can't tell anyone who you are?" she said, thumping a pillow and scowling angrily. "As if it has anything to do with her!"

"I can't believe she could be so mean!" Anita sighed. "I've got my coaching session with her tomorrow – I'm not going to enjoy it now!"

"Well, I'm just going to try and ignore her," I said bravely. But dear Diary, my heart sank as I remembered I had my coaching session with her coming up, too. The last thing I want is to be coached by Avocado Dieppe. I have too much to worry about already. My lines, for example! I can't believe we actually have to do the showcase next Saturday! If I think about it too much I start breathing quickly and panicking, so I am trying not to, and just to concentrate on learning my lines a little at a time, like Mrs. Howard told me, and—

Sorry about the interruption, dear Diary. There was a knock on the door and Trillian dived under her bed in case it was the cameras. But it was only Sarah, telling Anita it was time to go back to her own dorm, and for us to go to sleep.

Anita went off unhappily. She doesn't like

Heather Dorm, not since Isabel stole her bracelet. She spends all her time up here, which is okay with me and Trillian!

o   o   o   o   o   o   o   o   o

Day Nine
Monday.

Oh, dear Diary, the first full rehearsal today
was chaos! There were cameras and wires
everywhere, and hardly any room on the stage
for us.

Avocado was in the wings with Smoochy
Woo the whole time, and she was supposed
to be watching and helping direct only she
didn't, she just kept yawning and checking
her phone. Mrs. Howard was doing all the
directing work, and I think if it wasn't for her,
nothing would have gotten done at all.

Charlie was in the middle of his scene, and
had just put on the papier-mâché donkey's
head (which was REALLY hard to make, dear
Diary, and all of us helped), when Smoochy

Woo suddenly jumped out of Avocado's arms and ran onstage and started snarling at him!

Charlie couldn't see very well (we have to do something about the eyeholes) and so he was blundering around trying not to step on him, and other people were shouting at Smoochy Woo, and Avocado was shouting at Charlie, and Mrs. Howard got really angry and said, "Please remove that animal from the theater!" and some people got confused and thought she meant the donkey and started dragging Charlie off the stage, and Avocado got in a really bad mood and stomped off with Smoochy Woo. After the rehearsal, I could hear her on the phone all the way down the hall, telling her agent she wanted a helicopter sent to take her away, but it seems he wouldn't – huh.

Charlie got to do a big piece on camera stressing about it all, so he was happy in the end. But later on it turned out that some small animal, and we can't prove it was Smoochy Woo, has chewed up the papier-mâché donkey's head so one ear is not all it should be.

I have a BIG sense of foreboding, dear Diary. As if something dreadful is going to happen...

Later.

I was right!!!

In the afternoon we had to have a group photo taken in front of the Hall, with Avocado and Mrs. Howard at the center of the group.

We were all in our costumes, and the camera people said the photo might go into *Young Fame!*

(I think Mrs. Howard is not pleased with Avocado. The cameraman kept telling them to look more friendly, but it didn't seem to be working.)

I was right at the front because I'm one of the youngest and shortest, and I kept being sort of shuffled right in front of Avocado, which was really annoying. Then just as the photo was about to be taken, she let out this screech which nearly made my ears pop.

"Smoochy! My darling! He's got to be in the photo! You – bring him here!"

One of the film crew scurried away and came back with Smoochy Woo, holding him at arm's length. He handed him over to Avocado.

"But *I* can't hold him. He'll spoil the composition of the shot. Let me see—" She glanced down at me.

Oh nooo…! I thought. Avocado gave me an evil grin.

"Why doesn't this little girl hold him? That will be so sweet, don't you think?" She pushed Smoochy Woo into my arms.

"But—" I tried to push him back. He growled at me. "I don't think he likes me!"

"Just for a moment," said the cameraman. "Go on, it'll look great!"

I sighed and nodded.

"Ready?" shouted the cameraman. "Hold the dog up a little more, what's yer name – higher – that's great! Now smile everyone—"

FLASH!

Smoochy Woo let out a frightened *yip*!
I heard an awful trickling noise and felt something warm and wet seeping into my costume…

Smoochy Woo had peed!

All over my Puck costume!!

All over ME!!!

"Grooosss!" I shrieked.

I dropped Smoochy Woo and tried desperately to pat myself dry. Isabel and her friends were practically wetting *themselves* with laughter. Avocado clapped a hand over her mouth and said, "Oh no!!" but I could tell she was laughing under her hand.

Thank heavens Anita and Trillian were there!

They hurried me off to the dorm, and they got me out of the Puck costume and they washed it in the sink. It looked like a leaf that had gone through a horrible storm by the time they'd finished with it. I nearly cried!

You know the only reason I didn't? It was because everyone was SO NICE. Mrs. Howard said, "I'm terribly sorry, Bathsheba. I will have a word with Avocado about her dog." And Sarah and Josh came up to see if I was okay, and Sarah took the costume away to send it to the cleaners and said, "It'll be as good as new tomorrow, I promise!" And lots of people I didn't even know I knew came and knocked on the dorm door to ask if I was okay. Charlie said, "Don't worry, Bath. Hey, don't tell anyone this, but," he whispered, "I actually wet myself onstage in the school play! That's worse, right? But I was only six," he added hastily.

I gave him a wobbly smile. He's really kind.

"I hate Smoochy Woo!" I said to Trillian when everyone had gone and it was just us two.

"Hate is a very strong word," she said, "but yeah, me too!"

Later, later.

Uh-oh, dear Diary. Something rather worrying has happened.

After the horrible photo shoot, we all had to go and have individual interviews with the

Dramarama Diaries directors and do an intro piece on camera to say who we are and why we love acting and all that.

I was really excited about it. I'd even made myself a sort of script, but the moment I was sitting there looking into the camera – and even getting some powder put on my nose by a member of the film crew, just like a professional! – it all went out of my head. I was just so excited! I even forgot about being peed on.

The interviewer was a woman with a big nose. She smiled at me. "I'm Margaret, the director," she told me. "Are you excited to be here?"

I nodded violently.

"Fantastic – so are we!" She glanced down at a piece of paper. "What's your name?"

"Bathsheba Cl – Smithee," I said.

She gave me a very curious look. I turned red. I couldn't help it.

"I've got a list of the students registered here. There's no Bathsheba Smithee on the list. But there is a Bathsheba Clarice de Trop. It's not a common name!"

I didn't know what to say. So I didn't say anything.

"You couldn't be – by any chance – the daughter of the author..."

I felt myself getting redder and redder. I wasn't sure if I wanted her to find out or not, dear Diary. I did want to somehow get the better of Avocado! I hated the idea of her making me be anonymous! But was it worth it, if it would spoil Mother's movie?

"I knew it!" Margaret said triumphantly. "Fantastic! This will make a great show. The real Bathsheba Clarice de Trop and the actress who plays her, together at Dramarama camp – wow, what a story!"

"Oh no, please don't!" I gasped. "I mean – I don't want people to think I just told you who

I was because I wanted to get attention. And I...I think it could be confusing. You know – for the movie."

Margaret looked really disappointed, but she nodded. "Of course, we won't mention it if you'd rather not..."

Dear Diary, it's so annoying. I'm almost sure Avocado is just making this confusion thing up because she doesn't want to share the spotlight. But what if she's right? I don't want to spoil Mother's movie! She worked so hard to make it happen. And, also, I'm a little worried about what Avocado might do if I told everyone who I was...

One good thing is that my costume is fixed. It looks almost as good as new now that Sarah's dried it off.

o o o o o o o o o

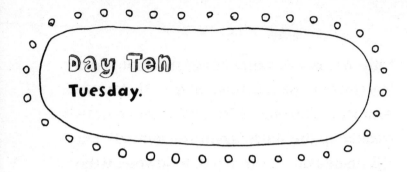

Oh no, dear Diary! A new DISASTER! And a completely unexpected one, too.

I was woken up by a loud doggy yelp and a huge CRASH. I sat up, blinking sleepily. Trillian was sitting up too, rubbing her eyes.

"What was that?" she yawned.

"I don't know! Let's go and see."

We went out into the corridor. The Assistants were coming out of their dorms, yawning and in their pajamas. That's when I heard it – someone groaning in pain! I ran to the top of the main stairs and looked down. I gasped in horror.

"Mrs. Howard!"

She was lying at the bottom of the stairs

with her leg at a horrible angle. She looked really white. As I stared at her in shock, she moaned, "The dog...I tripped..." and pointed weakly up the stairs. Then she fainted!

I rushed down the stairs, followed by the Assistants. Everyone was crowding out of their dorms on the floor below as well, and it was chaos, especially because the cameras turned up out of nowhere and were filming everything. (Margaret was jumping for joy and shouting, "Excellent story! Fantastic emotion!") Finally one of the Assistants yelled, "Go back into your rooms! She needs some air!"

Me and Trillian were herded back upstairs by Sarah while a cameraman filmed Josh calling for an ambulance.

As we went back upstairs Avocado was just coming out of her room. (Wow, dear Diary, I have never seen anything as pink as her dressing gown!)

"What's going on?" she demanded. "And has anyone seen Smoochy Woo?"

I looked around. Smoochy skulked past the top of the stairs, looking very guilty, and let Avocado scoop him up into her arms.

I exchanged a glance with Trillian. Dear Diary, it was pretty obvious what had happened! Poor Mrs. Howard had fallen over Smoochy Woo and gone straight down the stairs.

"That dog," said Trillian as we went back in to get dressed, "is a NIGHTMARE!"

Later. 6 ☆

Well, I am glad to say that Mrs. Howard is not dangerously hurt, but she has broken her leg and has had to be taken to the hospital. That was kind of exciting! The ambulance came along going *nee-naw, nee-naw,* and paramedics rushed out and took her away on a stretcher. (A cameraman went with her, and another one filmed him going.)

But everything is chaos here! Mrs. Howard was so important to the showcase! She was making sure everything got done, while Avocado wasn't helping at all. And none of the Assistants are really second-in-command, so no one really knows what we should do next.

o   o   o   o   o   o   o   O   o

Oh noooo... Dear Diary, baaaaaad developments...

Guess who's announced she's going to take over as director of the showcase – Avocado!

She told us all at breakfast. The Assistants looked a little uncertain, but the thing is, Avocado is the only professional actress here, now that Mrs. Howard is gone. The Assistants are still drama students, even if they've been in lots of shows.

"I have always wanted to direct!!" Avocado said, pointing one of her dazzling smiles at the nearest camera. "This will be a fantastic opportunity to show you all how we do it in Hollywood."

"But it's not a Hollywood movie," Anita muttered to me, "it's our showcase!" She looked really worried. "What if she spoils it?"

I took a deep breath. I didn't feel very happy about it either, but I could see there wasn't anything I could do about it.

"We'll just have to go on and do the best we can," I said firmly. "She can't make us act badly, however hard she tries!"

Later. Mid-morning break.

Oh no, I've just seen the schedule and today is my individual coaching lesson with Avocado.

I feel like crying, dear Diary. To think how excited I was about getting my private coaching from the Mystery Guest Star! Huh!

Oh well, off I go. Maybe I really will learn something, who knows?

After the coaching session... *

That was the most horrible experience of my life!!!

Oh no, wait, being peed on by Smoochy Woo was the most horrible experience of my life... But this was still horrible too!

Avocado was so mean to me!

I admit I was a little worried that she would be. But I kept telling myself: *I haven't done anything to upset her! I kept quiet about who I am, just like she wanted me to. Why should she be mean to me?*

I hadn't thought about the cameras at all, but there they were, in front of the rehearsal room door, waiting for me. I slowed down a little when I saw them. There was a cameraman, and there was Margaret, the director, the woman with the big nosy nose, who'd found out about my real name.

"Bathsheba!" she said excitedly, hurrying up

to me, her nose practically twitching. "Now –
I wondered if we could have just another little
talk before your session?"

"Um – sure," I said. I tried to smile at the
camera and act cool, but Margaret made me
nervous. I folded my arms and hugged my
script to me.

"It's about – you know – your secret identity."
She winked at the camera. "I know you don't
want to let people know – but if we recorded
some pieces on camera privately, so no one knew
until it was time to air..."

I felt as if the camera was looming at me. I
didn't know what to say. I wanted to be filmed,
but for my acting, not my name! And this director
woman was being really pushy. And Avocado—

"Excuuuuse me!"

Uh-oh, dear Diary. Avocado was standing
right behind me. I could see from her face that
she was furious.

"Talking to the cameras about your secret

identity?" she said to me, with a smile so sweet it made me want to brush my teeth.

"Ah ha!" said the director cheerily. (*Nothing seems to bother her, dear Diary, it's as if she's got feelings made of rubber or something!*) "I expect you know the exciting secret already! Will the real Bathsheba Clarice de Trop please stand up!"

Avocado tossed her hair, and as it fell across her face, between us and the camera, she gave me a furious glance and muttered, "I warned you!"

"It wasn't my fault," I began desperately. But Avocado just swept into the rehearsal room.

"Shall we get on with it?" she asked me. "It's not very professional to keep people waiting, you know, Bathsheba Whatever-You-Call-Yourself."

Dear Diary, that was a HORRIBLE coaching session!

I prepared for it really well, too! I'd learned

my Puck speech so I could say it backward. Huh, stupid me to think she'd care!

She let me go through the whole thing without a single comment. But when I got to the end – well, she was just horrible!

"You're a sprite, Bathsheba, a woodland fairy – not, like, an elephant! Have you ever noticed the way you walk? It's just so…so… clumsy. Really, you can learn your lines as well as you like, but you've got to think about acting with your body as well, you know."

DD, I had been so focused on learning my lines perfectly that I hadn't really been thinking about movement. But Mrs. Howard had never said I moved like an elephant! And Anita would have told me if I needed to change the way I moved…wouldn't she? Suddenly I wasn't sure anymore. I looked down at my feet anxiously. I could feel all my confidence draining out of me.

"But…but no one else said my movement was wrong," I said faintly.

Avocado smiled and glanced at the camera.

"Sometimes it takes a new eye to point these things out," she said. "I'm sure with a few weeks to practice, you'll have it down perfectly. Oh – but of course –" she made a worried face – "you don't have a few weeks, do you? You only have three days. Oh well. I'm sure it'll be okay…" She bent over her script. "Try it again – and this time, think about your movement! Remember – the cameras are watching."

So I did try it again, but I was just so worried about all of Britain seeing me walking like an elephant, dear Diary, that it was worse than the first time.

I got to the end and Avocado just looked at me, and then said, "Never mind. I'm sure it'll be all right on the night!"

She didn't give me any advice about how to do it better.

And now I feel all shaky and uncertain and worried, and I didn't feel worried before.

Of course, I know she is just being horrible because she thinks I told the director about who I really am. But she is a good actress even if she's horrible! If she says I'm no good then, well, maybe I'm really *not* any good!

Trillian says I'm being silly, but it's all right for her, she just has to stand still and be covered in flour.

What if the whole of the country sees me being awful on TV?

What if Keisha is disappointed? And Bill? And Mother?

I almost want to just give up and run away. Dramarama camp has gone all wrong now that Avocado is here!

After dinner.

I can't believe it! Avocado has cut lines from my final speech! It was my only long speech and she's hacked it to ribbons!

I didn't even know until it was time to go onstage during rehearsal. I was waiting in the wings, because when Charlie's scene finished the lights were supposed to go red and gold, and I was to come on and say my Puck speech. Well, the lights didn't change, but I ran onstage anyway. I started saying my lines.

"If we shadows have offended,
Think but thi—"

The boy who was prompting hissed, "That you have but slumber'd here."

I glared at him, irritated at being interrupted. "What are you talking about? That's the third line, not the second!"

"Read the new script, stupid!"

He tossed his script to me. I scanned it in

disbelief. There were red lines through half
my speech.

"But," I gasped, "that doesn't make any
sense now! It doesn't even rhyme!"

Anita, in the wings, looked as horrified as I
felt. I glanced up at Trillian, who was standing
on her pedestal. (It is really a stool with sheets
of cardboard around it.) She grimaced. Flour
drifted down into the spotlights.

"Oh, girls, didn't you get the new script?"
called Avocado from out in the audience.
I couldn't even see her for the blaze of the
footlights, but I could tell from her voice
she was grinning. "I thought I gave one to
everyone – so sorry – anyway, clear the stage
and we'll take it from the top with the love
scene."

Anita dragged me off the stage.

"Don't bother complaining," she said
angrily. "She just wants you to get upset. I'm...
I'm never going to watch her TV show again!"

The middle of the night.

We have just had an emergency meeting in the secret passage. I've read the whole script all the way through now. It's awful! She's cut random lines from my part! So now I have a script that makes me look as if I can't even remember my lines!

"I can't act this!" I said, almost in tears. "She's just trying to ruin it for me – I can tell!"

"We've got to complain to the Assistants," said Anita. "We'll do it tomorrow. Sarah likes us. She'll make Avocado change her mind."

"I'm not so sure," said Trillian grimly. "Did you hear the latest? Avocado wanted to light the stage with huge candles! She said it'd be romantic."

"But everyone knows you can't have naked flames on a theater stage!" I exclaimed. "It's a fire risk!"

"That's just what the Assistants tried to tell

her. She got really angry, though. I saw her shouting at Sarah and afterward Sarah looked as if she'd been crying. I think the Assistants don't want to get on the wrong side of Avocado either! They might *not* stick up for us."

We were sitting there miserably, with no appetite even for the three doughnuts we'd smuggled from morning break, when there was a snuffling noise and the door of the secret passage opened a crack. Something small rushed in, and next thing I knew, it was rushing out again – carrying Trillian's doughnut!

"Hey!" shouted Trillian furiously.

"Sssh!" me and Anita hissed. We rushed to the door. There was Smoochy Woo, savaging the doughnut in the middle of Trillian's bed. I glanced at the dorm door. We'd left it open by mistake.

"MY doughnut!" said Trillian furiously.

She rushed out to rescue it, but Smoochy Woo started growling and barking wildly.

"Oh no! He'll wake the Assistants up!" I gasped.

We hurried out of the secret passage, dragging our blankets behind us. We shut the door to the passage and shoved Trillian's bed back against it. Just in time!

The dorm door opened all the way and in rushed Sarah and Avocado, both looking as if they'd just been woken up. Smoochy Woo jumped off the bed in a shower of crumbs and scampered over into Avocado's embrace.

"What's happening?" Sarah demanded angrily. "Anita? What are you doing up here?"

"Um..." Anita looked frightened.

"She was just...we were just...practicing our lines," I said wildly.

"At this time of night! Honestly, have you no sense? Anita, go back to bed at once!" Sarah looked at our hands. "And sugar! Have you been keeping doughnuts to eat in bed?"

We glanced at each other.

"I'm really not happy! You've got just three days till the showcase – you need your sleep, not sugar in the early hours!"

We nodded shamefacedly, and Anita slunk out of the door and hurried off down the stairs.

"Now go back to bed, you two," Sarah grumbled, padding back out of the dorm.

Avocado followed her, but not before giving me a smug smirk, dear Diary!

"Ooh, she is so glad we're in trouble!" whispered Trillian when we were sure they had gone.

What with Avocado and Smoochy Woo, I don't know how I'm going to get through the last few days of Dramarama camp, dear Diary!

o　　o　　o　　o　　o　　o　　o　　o　　o

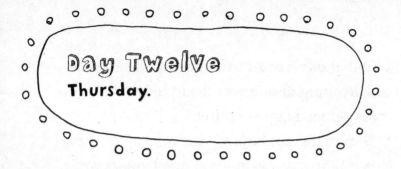

Day Twelve
Thursday.

I tried to complain to Sarah about my script being cut, but she is still upset with me, Trillian and Anita about last night.

I feel really upset! It's as if no one is listening. Even the cameras are busy following Avocado around. It seems as if all she has to do is throw a tantrum to get their attention. At this rate, *Dramarama Diaries* will be all about her!

And really annoyingly, she has moved into Mrs. Howard's room. It's the biggest on the floor, and it has an en-suite bathroom. I can smell Avocado's bubble bath all the way down here, and I'm sure she has scented candles even though there are notices everywhere saying they're not allowed because of the fire risk. At least she's given up the idea of having them on the stage – I think.

Later.

Trillian is in a huge rage. You'll never guess what – Avocado's found out who Trillian's dad is, and she wants to sing a duet with him!

She told Trillian so in her coaching session.

"And she kept going on about how she wanted to make an album and this was the perfect opportunity, and how it would be good for Dad as well because he'd get younger fans – YUCK!!!" stormed Trillian. "And it was all in front of the cameras too – the girls at school are never going to stop teasing me!" She stomped up and down. "And she's given me lines!"

"What – like lines to write out as a punishment?"

"No! Lines to say. Onstage." Trillian flumped down on the bed miserably, clutching her guitar like a favorite teddy bear. "She just didn't listen when I told her I didn't want a speaking part."

"So – is she *going* to duet with your dad?!"

"Not if I can help it!"

Bedtime.

Trillian is still really furious, dear Diary. "I'll show her!" she growls whenever I try to talk to her.

Oh, why did Avocado have to be the Mystery Guest Star? Everything has gone horrible since she turned up! I don't have a hope of being talent-spotted on *Dramarama Diaries* now that my speech has been cut. I know the director would film me talking about being Bathsheba Clarice de Trop, but if I do

that, Avocado will just be even nastier to me.
And besides, no one will notice my acting,
they will just want to know all about Mother.
And what if that does ruin the movie?

I just wish I wasn't here.

o   o   o   o   o   o   o   o   o

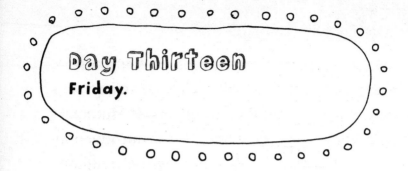

Dear Diary,
She's WRITTEN ME OUT!!!!

I can't believe it – with only one day to
go, too!!

And what's even worse is she's taken over
the compèring herself!!

When I got to the dress rehearsal today,
I could tell something was wrong at once.
Because there was Avocado, standing in
the middle of the stage. She was wearing a
HUGE deep green Elizabethan dress with
jewels all over the skirt, and a starry Alice
band just like mine only much, much starrier.
Oh, and a pair of gauzy wings. She looked
like a sofa crossed with a fairy godmother.

And she was performing the introduction that I wrote! Trillian was standing on her pedestal looking really uncomfortable, and not with a serene statue smile on her face at all.

"Follow me, fair gentlefolk, on this Midsummer night of magic, into a statue's dream..." I heard her say.

I didn't interrupt, because you shouldn't interrupt someone else's scene no matter HOW angry you are, but as soon as the lights went up, I marched right up onto the stage, and said, "Excuse me, but those were my lines! I actually wrote them!"

Avocado is an awful lot taller than me, dear Diary, and she was wearing high heels, too. She sort of batted her eyelashes at me, and said, "Oh, I made a few changes!"

"Changes?!" I spluttered.

"Yes! I think it would make the show so much more credible if someone really famous were to compère it. Don't you think? I mean, which would you rather watch – *The Statue's Dream*, a showcase compèred by Someone You've Never Heard Of, or *The Statue's Dream*, a showcase compèred by Avocado Dieppe, star of the forthcoming movie, *Bathsheba Superstar*?"

"But," I said, "Dramarama camp is supposed to be about giving people who aren't famous a chance! People like...like me!"

Avocado glanced at the cameras.

"I know!" she said brightly. "That's why I've let you keep the final speech."

The final speech??

The final speech that doesn't make any SENSE since she cut half of it!

I am *sooooo* angry!

I wish something awful would happen

to her – I hate her, I hate her!

What's the point of me staying at Dramarama camp?! Avocado is just going to do everything she can to ruin the showcase for me! I don't even *want* to be part of it anymore – my only speech doesn't make sense.

I'm going to call Bill and ask him to take me home.

Later.

Bill won't come and pick me up!

He just doesn't understand. I begged him and begged him!

He did sound really worried, but he kept saying, "But Dramarama camp is your dream!"

"It *was* my dream! Now it's my nightmare!"

"Oh, Bath – you're always so melodramatic! It was only the other day you texted me to say how well it was all going. Look, you still have some lines, don't you? And there's just one day left of camp to go. I can see this girl isn't being very fair – but you're better than that. Can't you just be dignified and mature and ignore her?"

"I don't want to be dignified and mature!!" I wailed. "I want to go home!"

"But that would be giving up! You wouldn't want to do that, would you?"

He sounded so sad and disappointed that I muttered, "No."

"That's my girl! You know that this is a fantastic chance for you, if you really want to be an actress. So it's harder than you thought – so what? You'll show them! Go girl!"

Oh, dear Diary, he doesn't understand.

He thinks I'm making a big fuss about nothing.

He doesn't know how I feel!!!

Maybe he just can't be bothered to come and get me.

I wish I was *anywhere* but here!!!

Half an hour later — after a big talk with Trillian!

Well, dear Diary. I have a plan. I am going to show them!

It's not just my plan – it's Trillian's too. Actually it was Trillian's first, but when she saw me crying she told me all about it. And now it's our plan, together!

We have had enough!

We are fed up with being pushed around!

We are going to show them we are serious about being taken seriously!

We are going to run away!!!

Yes! Yes yes yes yes yes yes.

SO THERE.

Trillian already has a bag packed, with cookies and water and spare socks in case it takes a long time to get back to London, and her iPod and her phone, and some money and the flashlight she uses to read in bed.

"I've had enough of that Avocado woman!" she said. "She won't stop nagging me to call my dad and tell him we're best friends. As if!"

"But where are you going to go, if there's no one at home?"

"I'm going to my brother Han's music camp. He won't tell anyone. So, are you coming?"

I wavered. It was a scary idea. But on the other hand...

"Yes!" I said.

DD, I have a hard, cold, proud and important feeling inside me.

They will be sorry at how they treated me when they wake up and find me gone.

We asked Anita if she wanted to come too, but she said no.

"My parents would go nuts! But I think you're so brave," she said wistfully. "Are you going to leave a note?"

We actually hadn't thought of that, but it's a really good idea. So I have written this note:

DEAR DRAMARAMA CAMP,
   WE HAVE GONE AWAY AND IT IS ALL AVOCADO'S FAULT.
   DO NOT LOOK FOR US. YOU WILL NOT FIND US.
   WE FORGIVE YOU (BUT WE DO NOT FORGIVE AVOCADO).
   LOVE,
   TRILLIAN AND BATHSHEBA.

Trillian has got everything planned. We are going to sneak down the secret passage after lights out, and we are going to stow away in the back of the camera crew's van. They always go to the pub after we've all gone to bed and there's nothing left to film. We're going to jump out as soon as they get to the village, go to the train station and get a train to London!

This is going to be the biggest adventure of my life!

Late at night.

Dear Diary,
Our plan succeeded!

It nearly failed – because we nearly bumped into Avocado on the way out! I don't know what she was doing, but she was heading off to the theater even though it was practically the middle of the night. She was lugging one of her lime-green suitcases around with her – weird. Thankfully she seemed as intent on not being seen as we were!

I am writing this in the back of the van. The radio is on really loud and they're all chatting so we don't even have to worry that they might hear us whispering.

I wonder how long it will take to get to the village?

Ooh, we're slowing down! This is it! We're going to climb out.

Later.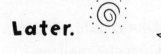

Oops, dear Diary.

It wasn't the village they were stopping at – it was a railroad crossing!

And by the time we realized we were in the middle of nowhere but fields, they'd driven off again!

It's really, really dark. But we are brave! We are marching down the road after the van. At least, we were. We've just stopped to have a cookie and put our spare sweaters on because it is COLD out here, so I'm taking the chance to tell you what's happened, DD. Oh, and the flashlight is really useless, it just shows a foot in front of you, which is okay to stop you from falling over cliffs but no good for seeing where you actually are.

Trillian says we have to get moving again, or we might freeze to death like explorers.

Write in you later, dear Diary. Hah! I hope Avocado feels really bad when she realizes we've gone.

Later. Having a break.

We've been walking for ages and ages and we haven't found the village yet. It's not as if I'm scared, but there are lots of funny noises in the dark and I don't know what they are...

Trillian started telling a story to cheer us up but it turned out to be a ghost story about a Great White Terror, so she stopped...but I keep thinking I see Great White Terrors in the fields, stalking us...

I really hope we find the village soon!

Later.

Ooh, a signpost!

It points out into the fields, and it says OZEBY BRITISH RAIL, 3 MILES.

Three miles can't be very far, can it?

Anyway, we are going down that path to find the train station!

Onward, brave diary!

Later.

I have just found the note in my pocket. All that, and we forgot to leave it!

Later. Sitting on a tree stump — at least, I hope it is a tree stump...

This is horrible!

There's no path anymore, just mud! And I think we are lost, and...I'm *sure* there are great white shapes looming in the mist like ghosts...

I will never go to the countryside again. I have learned my lesson! Oh, take me back to Clotborough!

Too tired to go on — sitting on a wet patch of grass...

I just got the fright of my life! This Great White Terror rose up out of nowhere and charged at us! I screamed, and Trillian screamed, and we dropped the flashlight.

It was a sheep.
It had been lying
in the middle of the
path. And it stepped
on the flashlight, so
now we don't have
any light except the
moon. I am writing
by the light of my
cell phone screen.

I hate sheep!

And I think they hate me too.

Thank heavens the moon is actually really
bright. And red. And seems to be shining from
behind that hill...

Hang on, that's not the moon! It must be
houses!

We're saved, dear Diary! We've found the
train station!

Later.

Oh, no!
   It's not the train station!
   It's Thespia Hall again!
   And – I think – it's on FIRE!!!!

o   o   o   o   o   o   o   o   o

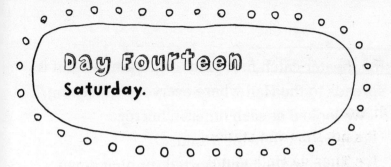

Day Fourteen
Saturday.

Well, dear Diary, I am writing this from a hospital bed. Yes, really!!!

I'm not badly hurt, don't worry! But I do smell as if I have been having the biggest barbecue in the world. Let me tell you all about it...

When we saw the fire, me and Trillian just stared at it in shock for a moment. We could see people moving around outside, and big searchlights swinging around from helicopters. I squinted hard at the flames.

"It's not the Hall that's on fire!" I exclaimed. "It's the theater!"

"You're right," said Trillian. "But how could

the theater catch fire? And – oh, Bath, what if it spreads to the Hall where everyone's sleeping?"

We looked at each other in horror.

"We've got to help!" I said.

Trillian nodded and started running down the hill toward the Hall. I followed her. NEVER try to run down a hill in the dark, dear Diary, you will just fall over and if you don't fall over you will go ten times faster than you expected to and end up rolling in a heap with your friend right into a crowd of astonished people, just like we did.

"Ow!" Trillian was clutching her ankle.

"Are you okay?" I asked her.

"I think I've twisted it," she gasped.

"Trillian! Bath!" Anita pushed through the crowd. "Why are you here? I thought—" She glanced around at the others and didn't say anything else.

"Long story," I told her quickly. "But what happened?"

"I don't know! The Assistants came around telling us that we had to get out, because the theater was on fire. It hasn't spread to the Hall yet, but it might at any moment! Josh and Sarah are just doing a roll-call now. I *think* everyone's out—"

There was a horrible scream from the Hall.

I turned around and so did everyone else.

Dear Diary – there, leaning out of her window and waving wildly, was Avocado, in a pink nightie!

A gasp went up from the crowd.

"Where are the firemen?" cried Trillian. She was still sitting on the ground, clutching her ankle.

"They're all at the Theater, trying to put out the fire. It's okay – all Avocado has to do is come down and she'll be fine," said Anita.

"Heeeelp!" cried Avocado. She disappeared from the window and then appeared at another window. "There's no way down!"

"But there is," said Anita. "The main staircase is fine, we all came down it!"

"Avocado!" we all yelled, jumping up and down and waving to her. "Come down the main stairs! But HURRY!"

Avocado disappeared from the window. We watched anxiously.

"She's coming down, she must be— Oh no, what's she doing back at the window?"

Avocado leaned out so far I was terrified she would fall. She seemed hypnotized by the flames coming out of the theater.

"I'm trapped!" she shrieked. "There's a FIRE!" she added.

By now everyone nearby was screeching "COME DOWN!!" and jumping up and down, too – except Trillian, who was sitting down, but she was shouting twice as hard as anyone so it kind of made up for it.

A figure rushed over to us. It was Josh, with his hair all everywhere and still wearing his pajamas. He was carrying a clipboard with a piece of paper and a pen.

"What's going on?" He saw me. "Bath! Finally! Thank heavens – I'll mark you off the register." He marked the paper on the clipboard.

"Avocado!" we all yelled at him, pointing up at the window.

Josh turned around. He saw Avocado. He actually staggered back in horror.

"Oh no!" he gasped. "What on earth is she still doing up there?" He cupped his hands around his mouth. "COME DOWN!"

"We've tried that," shouted Trillian, pulling at his pajama leg. He jumped back and looked down at her. "Oh, Trillian, good!" He made another mark on the clipboard.

Then there was a huge roar of flame from the direction of the theater, and a cloud of smoke rolled over the Hall. Avocado shrieked and reeled back into the room. We were all suddenly silent, gazing at the Hall. Thankfully when the smoke cleared, the Hall was still untouched.

"She's in a panic!" Anita said. "And every moment she stays up there it gets more dangerous. She'll be hurt if someone doesn't help her!"

I pointed silently. There were wisps of smoke curling out of the main door.

"The main stairs must be filling with smoke," said Josh grimly. "Honestly! If she had just come down when we told her to, instead of insisting on packing an overnight bag..."

My heart beat so fast, dear Diary. I had wished something awful would happen to her – and now it had! I felt so guilty.

"The secret staircase," I gasped.

"What?" said Josh.

I turned to him and tried to explain, my words falling over each other in my excitement.

"There's a secret staircase that leads up to

our dorm," I told him. "The door's behind that patch of ivy. If we go up that we can get to the top floor really quickly, and we can bring Avocado down it. It's safer than going up the main stairs because it's further from the theater."

Josh glanced at the Hall.

"I don't know, Bath. We should wait for the firemen..."

Avocado appeared at the window again, clutching a couple of handbags.

"I'm going to jump!" she cried dramatically.

"NOOOOOO!!!!" we all yelled.

Josh looked back at me. "Okay! I suppose we'll have to get her down before she injures herself. You'd better show me this staircase."

"Good luck!" yelled everyone behind us as we raced toward the Hall and the secret staircase.

Dear Diary, thank heavens Josh had a flashlight with him that hadn't been stepped on by a sheep. The secret staircase already smelled of smoke. We raced up, following the light as it bounced around on the walls and in the corners.

"It seems safe," said Josh, as we got to the top of the stairs. He shouldered the door into our dorm open. "Wow, Bath, you were right, this leads right to the top bedrooms! It must be the old servants' staircase."

"The what?"

"Well, in the old days when they had servants, they used to have special staircases for them to go up and down so they weren't always bumping into the elegant family – anyway, this is no time for a history lesson! Avocado!" he yelled as we went down the corridor toward her room. "We're coming! Don't worry!"

The door to Avocado's room was open, and

there was a half-packed lime-green suitcase on the bed – but Avocado was not there.

I stared at Josh and he stared at me. The same horrible thought filled both our minds and we rushed to the window and leaned out, terrified that Avocado really had jumped!

But, thank heavens, she hadn't.

In the distance, the crowd of children and Assistants were jumping up and down and waving. I saw one of them put her hands to her mouth and yell: "She's UP THERE!" and pointed above our heads – to the roof!

"Oh good grief!" Josh looked stunned. "How did she get up there? She must have gone through the attic – there's a trapdoor to the roof – but how can we go up there and get her?"

"The main stairs," I said.

We rushed down the corridor and to the main stairwell. But as we got closer, we saw it was getting smokier and smokier. We started coughing and gasping for air. Josh grabbed my arm.

"We can't go up there. The smoke could overpower us – we'd collapse."

"But we can't leave Avocado either!" I glanced at the main stairs, and distantly, I thought I heard the crackle of flames.

"Do you think the servants' passages might go right up to the attic?" I asked, without much hope.

"Of course! Why didn't I think of that – the servants' bedrooms were in the attic! You're a genius, Bath. Come on, back to your secret staircase!"

We rushed back to my dorm and into the secret staircase.

"We never really went the other way because there was so much owl poop and yuck and it looked like there was a wall there," I told him as he shone the flashlight into the other end of the passage just as we had done.

"It's not a wall." He rapped on it. "It's a door!"

We threw ourselves against the door – and dear Diary, we went straight through in a shower of old owl poop! Something ratlike scuttled away in fright as we fell through, but I didn't have time to be scared.

Josh shone his flashlight ahead of us. Stairs led up...

"Wait!" I said. "I can hear something..."

Faintly, we could hear Avocado screaming.

"Smoochy Woo!" she was wailing. "Smoooooooochy!"

We ran up the stairs toward her voice, and found another old door which led into the attic. It was a long, narrow room with a sloping ceiling. At the far end of it, there was a newer door – the normal way in from the main stairs – and just in front of that a trapdoor to the roof hung open, and through it the light from the burning theater shone. We could hear helicopters chopping overhead and the crackle of flames.

"Stay here," said Josh firmly. "The floor might not be safe." He handed me the flashlight and went carefully through the attic, and shone his flashlight up through the trapdoor. "Avocado?" He stuck his head through so he could look around the roof for her, then leaned out further. I saw him struggling and then I saw Avocado's legs in her pink nightie being helped down through the hole.

"I've got you. You're safe! Come on, we have to get out of here," Josh was saying as he let her down.

"But Smoochy Woo!" she gasped. "I lost him – I couldn't find him! He ran up here and into the attic and I lost him down the other end of it. I can't leave without him!"

I glanced behind me, suddenly remembering the ratlike thing that had scurried away when we'd fallen through the door in the secret passage...

I turned around and went back down the stairs. I thought of telling Josh about it, but I knew it would be quicker to find Smoochy Woo myself.

"Smoochy!" I called. "Come out! Time to go!"

But he wasn't there. The smell of smoke was getting stronger. Surely it couldn't be long before the Hall was in flames around us? My chest was tight with terror. I had to find Smoochy Woo.

I went back into our dorm and searched under the beds.

"Smoochy!" I called. "Please!"

There he was crouching in the corner. He whimpered and snarled and tried to bite my fingers, but I grabbed him and rushed back to the attic. Just as I'd suspected, Josh and Avocado hadn't moved.

"You've got to leave AT ONCE!" Josh was shouting at her.

"Never without my Smoochy!" Avocado yelled back.

"I've got him!" I yelled, waving him above my head.

"Smoochy!" Avocado ran down the attic toward me. Smoochy leaped from my arms into hers, and licked her face. "Honey, you're safe – oh, and look! There are stairs here! We're saved, Smoochy! Saved!!" She hugged him tight.

Dear Diary – I suddenly realized that Smoochy Woo wasn't just a fashion accessory. Avocado really loved him! (Crazy, I know.)

We all rushed down the stairs as fast as we could. We tumbled out of the door at the bottom, through the ivy, and onto the grass. Firemen came running toward us. My eyes were sore with smoke, but I could see that the fire over at the theater had nearly been put out. It looked ruined, though!

Dear Diary, I remember a fireman putting

an oxygen mask on me, and I have one brief memory of being in an ambulance, and that's it. And then I woke up here – in the hospital. The nurse says that I'm perfectly fine but I've suffered from smoke inhalation and I need to rest. And she says the theater is wrecked but no one is really hurt. Actually, I am the most hurt person of anyone.

I'm exhausted now, dear Diary, and I still feel a little sick and cough-y, so I'm going to get some sleep before Bill comes to see me this afternoon.

Later. *

Wow, guess what, it wasn't just Bill who came to see me!

Keisha and Bev came too!

They got back last night!

YAAAAAAY!!!!!!

They brought me lovely flowers, and grapes.

We talked for ages – well, half an hour. And then Anita and Trillian came in, looking shy, with big bunches of flowers, and I was so happy I just squealed!

I introduced Keisha to Anita and Trillian and they said hello politely and it was really weird because of them all knowing me but not all knowing each other. But by the end of the visit they'd gotten to know each other and we were chatting as if we'd all been friends forever.

It seems that the fire was started by big candles that Avocado had put on the stage in the theater!

"No!" I exclaimed when Trillian and Anita told me. "After the Assistants told her how dangerous it was?"

"Yes, and there was an old sort of carpet too, or something, and that made it worse. But you know when we almost bumped into her on the way out to..." Trillian trailed off because, of course, no one except Anita knew that we'd tried to run away!

I nodded.

"Well, she was off to try out the candles without telling anyone – that's what was in the suitcase, there were about twenty of them – and she didn't put them out completely when she left."

"And now our theater's ruined!" I said angrily. "And what about the showcase?" An awful thought struck me. "Oh no – I hope the donkey's head hasn't gone up in flames! It took forever to make!"

"I thought you weren't so big on the showcase anymore?" said Bill. "After what you said on the phone."

I suddenly felt awful. Of course I cared

about the showcase! And yet I'd just run off without thinking about how it would let everyone else down. Just because I'd been upset about losing my part. And of course, it was supposed to happen tonight. Only now, everything was ruined because of the fire!

"We *can't* not do the showcase!" I cried. "Everyone worked so hard for it!"

Bill gave me a big hug.

"Don't worry about that now! The main thing is that you're safe."

I suppose he is right, but...I can't stop thinking about the showcase! It should be happening right now. Maybe we'll be able to do it later, when everyone has recovered from the shock of the fire. But how can we, with no theater to perform in?

Later, later.

Mother called! She sounded so worried, poor Mother.

"I can't wait for you to come and see me out here," she said. "Darling, I can never feel that you're completely safe without me!"

She cheered up as soon as I asked her about the movie, though. Apparently Avocado being in a fire has given it even more publicity! We talked for ages, and we arranged that I would go out and stay with her for two weeks as soon as I was better. Ooh, Hollywood, here I come!

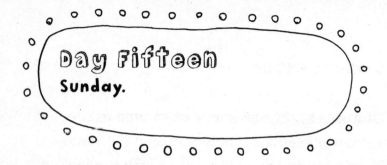

Dear Diary,

Oh wow!

Keisha woke me up this morning, and guess what she had with her?

She had a copy of Young Fame! magazine, and a copy of YAY! magazine, and a copy of some newspapers, and all of them had a picture of Thespia Hall in flames on the cover, and a picture of Josh, and, in the corner, a picture of me! (It's my school photo, which is a little uncool, but oh well.)

"BRAVE KIDS SAVE STAR," read Keisha. "REAL-LIFE BATHSHEBA IN DRAMA TRAUMA. Bath, you're famous!"

Later.

Ooh, dear Diary, Mrs. Howard came to see me!

I never realized that we were in the same hospital. She's in a wheelchair with her leg sticking out in front of her in a cast. She said I could be the first person to sign it, so I did my best Star Autograph with three kisses and a smiley.

"Mrs. Howard," I said, as soon as we'd gotten the polite parts out of the way, "what about the showcase?"

"Oh, we'll go ahead with it," she said cheerfully. "We sent an emergency e-mail around and people really want the show to go on. Even Avocado's staying on – the fire's brought her a lot of attention from the British press."

"But there's no theater."

"We'll do it outside next weekend. It's August, after all! The Assistants are already hard at work setting up an outside stage. The Hall has been cleared of smoke and all of the students have stayed on to be involved. It'll look great – and lots of people chipped in with support when they read about the fire in the newspapers. I think it's going to be a big success! Which reminds me – I brought along your script so you could rehearse!"

She handed me the old script, dear Diary. The script before Avocado changed it.

I looked at it and my heart sank.

"Um...I think Avocado might have made some changes," I said sadly.

"Oh really?" Mrs. Howard raised an eyebrow. (I really want to learn how to do that, dear Diary! I've been practicing, but both of them go up together.) "I'd heard some rumors... But don't worry about that. Just use that script for now."

o o o o o o o o o

One Week Later:
The Night of The
Showcase!

Dear Diary,

This is it! Finally!

I can't believe how wonderful the outdoor stage looks. I've just been helping set up the mattresses underneath it for when they do the flash-bang-disappear trick later on. The people from a local garden center have lent us lots of lemon trees in pots, so we have a real forest, and they've put garlands of roses and honeysuckle around the stage so it smells gorgeous, and there are going to be candles, only NOT on the stage, but those safe flat garden candles to help light the audience to their seats.

The stage is pretty high off the ground and it has steps at both ends to get up onto it. There are tiers of bench seats for the audience to sit on, so they have a really good view down onto the stage.

I've got to go backstage soon – really, under the stage! – to put my costume on, though it seems sort of pointless when I know I only have half a speech to do, right at the end.

Trillian is standing really still in the corner while Charlie pours bags of flour over her. She won't talk to anyone. She says she is getting into character.

And Anita looks wonderful! She is just gliding around looking like a perfect majestic dreamy Titania! She is wearing her jade bracelet, too.

Ohhh...I wish I was still the compère...

Got my costume on now — I feel so excited!

Avocado isn't here yet. I haven't seen her since the fire. Wait a minute, dear Diary! I haven't seen Mrs. Howard either! She said she'd be here... She *promised*...

Oh, wait, dear Diary! Here comes a limousine!

After the showcase.

Wow, dear Diary! That was the best night of my life!

I almost feel sorry for Avocado, though. Almost! Well, maybe not after the present she gave me...

I was hoping and hoping that it would be Mrs. Howard in the limousine. But it wasn't. The door of the limousine opened and out got a very tall, stylish man with glossy teeth like Avocado's. I could see his teeth because he smiled as he opened the door.

Out got Avocado. Well, to be exact, she got halfway out. Then she got stuck, because she was already wearing her huge green Elizabethan costume. The man gave her a pull and she popped out like a...a...I don't know, like an avocado out of a crowded fruit bowl.

She fussed about her costume a second, and made the tall man make sure her skirt wasn't ripped, and then, dear Diary, she came swooshing straight up to me! The *Dramarama Diaries* cameras followed her. I backed away into the shadow of the stage, but she cornered me.

"I want to thank you, *soooo* much, for rescuing my darling Smooch!" she told me. She really had tears in her eyes. "You don't

know what he means to me. He is my one true
friend."

"Oh, um, that's okay," I muttered. "It was
Josh who did it really, uh..."

"I have a gift for you," she said, batting her
eyelashes at the cameras.

For one huge hopeful moment, dear Diary,
I thought she was going to tell me she was
giving me my role back!

But no.

She gestured to the tall man, who handed
her a narrow box wrapped in sparkly paper.

"This is for you," she said. "It's an
exclusive!"

I took the box.

"Um...thank you," I said.

"Aren't you going to open it?" asked one of
the cameramen, whose face was totally hidden
behind his huge camera.

What else could I do, dear Diary? I was on
camera! I unwrapped the box.

It was a doll. A doll that looked horribly familiar. A doll that looked like…Avocado!

"Bathsheba Clarice de Trop Movie Tie-In Action Doll!" I read from the packaging. "Style My Hair and Help Me Save the World! I say Three Fantastic Phrases from the Movie!"

Avocado leaned over and pulled the doll's long blond hair.

"*I am Bathsheba Clarice de Trop!*" said a recorded voice from inside the doll. "*And My Life is Fantastic!!!*"

I was speechless, dear Diary.

Thankfully, I didn't have to say anything else, because just at that moment the music was turned up. The audience clapped and settled happily into their seats.

"That's my cue!" gasped Avocado. And she swept off toward the stage.

I watched her go. On the stage, Trillian was miming a scene with Charlie and another boy.

As the music reached a crescendo, Trillian froze into a statue.

Charlie and the other boy carried Trillian, who was being as stiff as possible, across the stage to her pedestal and heaved her up onto it – she did help them a little with that, but you couldn't tell unless you were standing close like me. Meanwhile, Avocado swept up onto the stage. A spotlight went onto her, and there was a round of applause from the audience. In her Elizabethan dress, she Glittered, dear Diary. She still looked like a sofa, but a very glamorous sofa.

I felt a pang of misery, dear Diary. It should have been me up there! I knew the words she was about to say by heart, and I whispered them along with her:

"Follow me, fair gentlefolk, on this Midsummer night of magic, into a statue's dream..."

Then, dear Diary, a *second* spotlight came on.

This one was pointing away from the stage to the ground at the back of the rows of benches. The audience *oohed* and *ahhed* and tried to see what was happening.

Avocado stopped in the middle of her line and looked confused.

"Hello – lights???" she snapped.

Someone was coming toward the stage, caught in the spotlight. Someone was *rolling* toward the stage, dear Diary! It was Mrs. Howard in her wheelchair! She was wearing a costume of a wizard's robe covered in moons and stars, and she was holding a long silver wand. She looked amazing!

She got right up in front of the stage and wheeled to face the audience.

"Uh, I don't think this is in the script," said Avocado.

The audience laughed. Dear Diary – I knew it wasn't in the script either! But *they* didn't. I turned to look at Anita, who was watching from behind me. She shrugged, looking puzzled. Trillian was peering down from her pedestal in a very non-statue way to see what was going on.

"Enter – Prosperina," said Mrs. Howard. Her voice rang out, clear and powerful. Even though she was in a wheelchair and wasn't actually on the stage, it was as if she was ten times taller than Avocado. "The sister of Prospero – and no less great a magician."

The audience gasped. I didn't blame them. She sounded so real. I almost believed her!

"The time has come to dismiss these shadows," Mrs. Howard gestured at Avocado, "and restore things to the way they should be." She added to Avocado, "Move slightly to your right, will you?"

The audience laughed. Avocado looked uncertain, but she shuffled to her right. Mrs. Howard just has that kind of voice, dear Diary.

"And – disappear!" Mrs. Howard pointed the wand at Avocado.

Flash! went the lights.

Bang! went the sound effects.

And – when we could see again and the audience had stopped squealing – Avocado was GONE!

I clapped a hand to my mouth in astonishment. From underneath the stage – on the pile of mattresses – I heard Avocado shrieking furiously.

Mrs. Howard raised her voice. "And now – on with the show!"

She beckoned to me. Me!!!

Anita reached out and grabbed the doll from me. I stepped forward, trembling.

"Onto the stage, dear," Mrs. Howard said quietly to me. "And just continue as normal. You know your lines, don't you?"

I nodded. I took a deep breath. Then I walked around to the steps and went slowly up them onto the stage.

I looked out over the audience. All I could see was a sea of faces, and for a moment I was terrified. What if I disappoint them? I thought. But then I saw one…two…three faces smiling back at me. Bill, and Keisha, and Bev.

"So follow me, dear audience," I heard myself saying, in a voice that was almost as clear and mysterious as Mrs. Howard's, "into a statue's dream…."

Oh, dear Diary, there were so many things to talk about afterward!

About how fabulous it had been and how it hadn't even mattered that one of the lemon trees fell over…

About how the audience had laughed and cried and clapped and even whistled at some parts!

About how the donkey head had lasted really well despite being a little smoked and had only fallen to pieces *after* Charlie's scene!

About how fantastic Anita's speech had been and how the audience had loved the dance she did afterward...

About how Trillian had heroically managed to stand almost totally still almost all the way through...

And everyone, even people I didn't know at all, kept coming up to me saying, "You were wonderful!" and "You really held the show together!" and "Which stage school do you go to?"

And finally, when most of the people had gone except the parents and the cameras and we had started to take down the stage, the most astonishing, unexpected, wonderful thing happened, dear Diary.

I was sitting on the edge of the stage winding up a lighting cable and Trillian was sitting next to me talking to Bill and Keisha. Anita was off with her dad, who kept telling everyone she was the best thing in the show, when suddenly I heard an American man's voice say, "Miss de Trop?"

I looked up in surprise. It was the tall man who had come with Avocado, and he was smiling at me with his glossy teeth.

"I believe you forgot this," he said, holding out the Bathsheba doll.

"Oh!" I said guiltily.

"But perhaps you're a little old for dolls," he said. "I know a great children's charity that would very much like to have it…"

"Oh, do you?" I said gratefully. "Oh good – I mean, it was very nice of Avocado, but…"

He raised a hand. "Say no more. I've been Avocado's agent since she was your age, and believe me, she was just the same back then. It's a pleasure to watch a show like this where no one's a diva. Still, it's possible that seeing herself on *Dramarama Diaries* may open Avocado's eyes a little. They say the camera never lies…"

"You're Avocado's *agent*?" I said. "*Theatrical* agent?"

"I am indeed."

He handed me a business card. This is what it said:

FREDERICK UNGERER

THEATRICAL AGENT

UNGERER AND UNGERER

197 SUNFLOWER BOULEVARD,

BEVERLEY HILLS, CA.

"There's a movie just going into casting that you might find interesting," he said as I stared at the card. "It's a contemporary teen version of Shakespeare's *A Midsummer Night's Dream* set in a high school – they're calling it *A Midsummer Night's Prom*."

"Oh," I said blankly. I couldn't believe that I was actually holding the business card of an actual theatrical agent. I wondered if he would let me keep it. Then I could stick it on my wall next to my picture of Connie Clyde and dream of the day when—

"...the part of the jock's best friend, the tomboyish Robyn Goodfellow. The role corresponds to Puck, the role you just handled so well."

I nodded, wondering why he was telling me all this.

He stopped and looked at me as if he expected me to say something. I looked around. For some reason Keisha and Bill and Trillian were all staring at me with slightly insane expressions too.

"Um, it sounds like a really good movie," I said. "I'll definitely go and see it when it comes out."

There was a huge silence. Then Keisha leaned over and gave me a shove.

"Bath, you dope!" she squealed. "He's offering you the chance to AUDITION for it!!!"

Dear Diary, for the first time in my life, I think I can honestly say: "My life is FANTASTIC!"

o o o o o o o O o

My Top Ten Tips for Being a Super-Starry Stage Success

1) If you've got a huge long speech to learn, don't panic! Just concentrate on getting the first two lines memorized. Then, when you can remember them, move onto the next two lines. It's much easier to learn it bit by bit.

2) Try out different ways of saying your lines. Sometimes a well-placed Wobble can make your speech sound more interesting.

3) If you ever have to make a mask of a donkey's head for a play, make it really strong, because you have no idea what might happen to it. (Charlie suggested that one.)

4) Remember acting isn't just about talking, it's about movement too — if you're supposed to be acting an elephant, don't scurry around like a mouse!

5) Don't be afraid to Pause. A little bit of silence will make the audience sit up and listen to you.

6) It's no use remembering your lines if no one can hear you say them! Remember to speak up — not shout! — so the people in the back row can hear you. One of them might just be a theatrical agent!

7) Improvisation can seem scary — but it's REALLY good fun when you get into it.

8) If you're having trouble getting into character, think about MOTIVATION. Motivation means what your character wants and needs. Understanding their motivation will help you get into their head.

9) If you have to be a statue, or a corpse, or something that is onstage for ages without moving, make sure you get yourself into a comfortable position right at the start, because you can't fidget when you're supposed to be made out of stone! (Trillian suggested that one.)

10) Share the spotlight — I know it's hard, but it's the nice thing to do! Being a super-starry actress is important, but so is having friends!

☆ About the author ♭ ✳

Like Bathsheba's mother, Mandy de Trop, Leila Rasheed is a writer. Unlike Mandy, Leila lives in Birmingham, England. This is not as glamorous as Kensington in London, but it does have a suburb called Hollywood!

Here are some more differences between Mandy and Leila:

☆ Mandy has a diamond-encrusted swimming pool to splash around in.
☆ Leila just has a bathtub to splash around in, which is lucky, as she loves bubble-baths (and Bathsheba!).

☆ Mandy rides around in swishy, dishy limousines.
☆ Leila rides around on buses and trains. She loves walking too — you can explore a lot more on foot than from behind the tinted windows of a limo.

☆ Mandy has a housekeeper to clean up after her.

☆ Leila lives with a saxophonist, who sometimes cleans up, but mostly makes weird and wonderful music.

☆ Mandy writes in a perfectly white office, where nobody is allowed to touch anything in case it gets dirty.

☆ Leila writes in a jumble of computer cables, cookie crumbs and half-empty mugs of tea.

☆ Mandy is often to be found surrounded by fans pleading for her autograph.

☆ Leila is often to be found surrounded by notebooks full of scribbled ideas for new stories, silently pleading to be written.

With thanks to Phoebe Wilkinson for the title.

First published in 2009 by Usborne Publishing Ltd., Usborne House,
83-85 Saffron Hill, London EC1N 8RT, England.
www.usborne.com

Inside illustrations by Vicky Arrowsmith.
Illustration copyright © Usborne Publishing Ltd., 2009

A CIP catalogue record for this book is available from the British Library.

UK ISBN 9780746098844 First published in America in 2011. AE.

American ISBN 9780794530303 JF AMJJASOND/11 00181/1

Printed in Reading, Berkshire, UK.